THE RESCUE

EDGE OF THE WORLD SERIES : BOOK TWO

LEROY A. PETERS

PROLOGUE

LATE MAY OF 1828

Belly River, Northwestern Montana

Summer was right around the corner, but for the village of Chief Buffalo Hump, it felt like it had already arrived. Not that anyone was complaining, for today had been a good day. The people had had a successful hunt and brought down many buffalo from a very large herd. Tonight, there would be a feast fit for a royal family for the entire village.

Buffalo Hump and his younger brother, Kills The Enemy, shared the strong enthusiasm of their people. However, there was a lot to think about, and plans needed to be made for the future. Summer was the time the warriors, led by their great and feared war chief and his evenly more feared younger brother, would go on a raid against their many enemies, such as the Crow, Nez Perce, Flathead, Shoshone, Lakota,

Cheyenne, Arapaho, Assiniboine, and the Cree. The tribe that the people belonged to was none other than the Blackfoot Confederacy. Along with their allies the Atsina (called Gros Ventre by the trappers), they were the most feared and deadly tribe of the Northern Plains and the Rocky Mountains. Their hatred and distrust of the white man were legendary, ever since Meriwether Lewis of the Lewis and Clark Expedition murdered two Blackfoot teenagers at the Medicine River back in 1805. Since then, the Confederacy and their allies had it in for all trappers and white men and anyone who traded with them.

The Confederacy consisted of three main clans. The Pikuni (Piegan), Siksika (Blackfoot proper), and the Kainai (Bloods). The Kainai, of which the village of Buffalo Hump were members of, was considered the most feared out of all the three clans, with Buffalo Hump the most feared and well respected among the people. He was considered more level-headed than his brother and a terrific strategist. It was for this reason alone the people followed him. However, like most tribes, the Blackfeet didn't have a single chief who ruled over an entire nation. Each village in a tribe was ruled by a council of elders, and Buffalo Hump's village was no exception. However, the elders themselves had great respect for the war chief, who was in his late thirties but still had the features and vitality of a much younger man. His reputation as a leader and his love for his people and family served him well.

While Kills The Enemy wasn't as judicious as his older

brother, that didn't mean he was a hothead. He was the exact opposite and was even humble compared to most men of his stature and reputation. It was because of this that the brothers were very close and would often confide in each other when it came to decisions about the village, the hunt, their enemies, and their families.

Another thing the two brothers had in common was that they were devoted husbands and fathers. Chief Buffalo Hump and his wife had a son named Heavy Eagle, now in his eighteenth summer, and two daughters, seventeen-year-old She Bear Woman, and fifteen-year-old White Flower. While polygamy was a common practice among the Blackfeet, Chief Buffalo Hump was satisfied with his one and only wife, Little Bird. However, Kills The Enemy had two wives, Snow Bird and Thunder Cloud Woman, and between them he was the father of five sons and one daughter. Star Watcher was his daughter by Snow Bird, his primary wife, and she was also his eldest child by her; they had a total of three children together.

Star Watcher was the same age as White Flower, and the three girls were close as their fathers were close. There wasn't a thing the trio didn't get into, led by She Bear Woman. There was always fun and games to get into and people to play pranks on, much to the detriment of their parents. While the festivities were in play, She Bear Woman and White Flower were seeking out their partner in crime, after they filled their bellies.

"Where could Star Watcher have gone?" asked White Flower.

A sly grin came across her sister's face. "I am betting Dog Star finally managed to get her to be alone with him by the willows."

White Flower giggled a little before giving a more serious look. "You better not let Uncle Kills The Enemy hear you say that," she said. "You know how overprotective he is."

"Can you blame him?" asked She Bear Woman. "I mean, what kind of man would be knocking on a girl's lodge flap in the middle of the night?"

"A man who is not too fond of living," said White Flower. "As far as Uncle Kill The Enemy is concerned."

The two sisters laughed as they strolled towards the river since that was where Star Watcher was last seen. Once they got there, they were so entranced into their discussion, they didn't realize the four silent strangers hiding in the bushes. Two of them held an unconscious Star Watcher bound and gagged as they prepared to pounce on the two unsuspecting would-be victims. By the time the girls saw them, it was too late.

Twenty miles southwest of the village lay a camp. There were at least twenty men. Sixteen of them were Indian, members of the Ute tribe, whose territory was way south beyond that of the Yellowstone River, which was Crow country. Their territory was in what is now known as the states of Utah and Colorado, so they were a long way from home.

However, the men leading them were the four white men who put this whole expedition together. They were Charles Bundy, Ted Gacy, Richard "Dick" Dahmer, and Boston Chapman.

Charles Bundy was the ringleader of this party of ex-trappers turned kidnappers. They had been at it for the previous two years, kidnapping Indian women and children from different tribes up and down the Rocky Mountains and selling them as slaves to the Mexicans. The Ute Indians historically were notorious for doing this, which is one of the reasons the quartet hired them and managed to put this group together.

While Bundy was the ringleader, Dahmer was the most psychotic and lust-crazed. Gacy and Chapman was more prudent and had a bit more common sense but were terrified of Bundy and his right-hand man—Dick Dahmer.

Among the Ute warriors that accompanied this party, Red Knife was the leader and could speak both English and Spanish and often talked with Bundy and Dahmer, despite the fact he didn't trust them anymore he could throw them, and the feeling was mutual; however, both men believe that the partnership was beneficial. Raiding into Blackfoot country to kidnap women (and children, if possible) gave a kind of sudden thrill to the Ute, and he made no secret about it. That was one of the reasons Charles Bundy liked him.

The only men in this party who thought going into the Blackfoot country for any reason was beyond madness were

Gacy and Chapman. However, Dahmer let them both know if they objected, the Blackfeet would be the least of their worries.

"Running Horse comes," said Red Knife.

Out of the darkness rode four other Ute, along with three Blackfeet captives, one tied over each horse and gagged.

Charles Bundy was impressed. "My, my," he said. "Now that is an impressive catch."

Running Horse spoke to Red Knife in the Ute tongue before the older warrior translated. "He says these two," he said, pointing at She Bear Woman and White Flower, "are the daughters of the Blood chief, Buffalo Hump."

"Holy smokes!" shouted Chapman. "We need to get the hell out of here right now!"

"Shut your trap, you stupid idiot," threatened Dahmer.

Charles Bundy calmly took control of the situation. "He does have a point, my friend," he said. "We are deep in Blackfoot country after all, and now that we have what we came for, we should be headed to safer pastures."

"Don't tell me that you are scared of the Blackfeet," said Dahmer.

Bundy scoffed. "Dick, my friend," he said, "since when have you known me to be scared of any man?"

"Well, I'm terrified," said Ted Gacy. "Coming into Blackfoot country was bad enough, but kidnapping two daughters of the most feared Blackfoot chief, that is insane."

Now Bundy as well as Red Knife were getting annoyed.

"If it makes you feel better," said Bundy, "we are hightailing it out of here right now."

"Where to, boss?" asked Dahmer.

"We'll ride south, then turn east to the Powder River, towards Cheyenne Country," answered Bundy.

A wicked grin came upon Dahmer's face. "I have always wanted to snag me a Cheyenne gal."

"Well, you just might get your chance, my friend," responded Bundy as he had everyone saddle up and ride out with their three captives.

1

Mountain Man Rendezvous, Sweet Lake, Utah

The fourth annual Mountain Man Rendezvous was in full swing. Trappers, fur traders, and Indians alike were getting ready to sell and trade their furs to resupply for the following year. Stories would be told of the last two trapping seasons and news shared of who made it and who went under. The life of a trapper was a dangerous one. Anything could happen, from hostile Indians, other trappers who would rob and kill their fellow man without thinking twice, Mother Nature, vicious beasts, and accidents. For every ten days, one trapper would die or be killed in just one season. Even veterans, who lasted more than two years, sooner or later succumbed, if they decided to stay in the wilderness and practice their trade.

The Rendezvous was an annual summer gathering for trappers lucky enough to survive the winter and spring trapping seasons to not only sell their plews and resupply themselves, but to let loose and have fun. The first Rendezvous took place in June 1825 in Ham's Fork in what is now the state of Wyoming. Started by William Ashley, owner and founder of the Rocky Mountain Fur Company, the first Rendezvous lasted only one day. But the following ones would last at least the entire summer, depending on if and when the supply train arrived. Since Ashley sold the company to trappers Jedediah Smith, William Sublette, and David Jackson in 1826, the Rendezvous had been considered the most successful system in the fur trade, saving trappers time and money. They no longer had to leave the mountains and travel to St. Louis or to the many forts on the frontier to sell their plews and outfit themselves.

It was also safer for them, but there was a tradeoff. Since Ashley provided the supplies to trade and had to travel from St. Louis to the designated rendezvous site, the company charged extremely high prices for their supply and trade goods. For example, a bag of coffee beans would cost twenty cents a pound in St. Louis, but at Rendezvous, they would cost a trapper between $1.50 and $2 a pound. There would be nothing that the trappers could do about it, even if they had two great trapping seasons. The money they made from their plews didn't go far, and they would still end up almost broke from buying supplies and such.

Many tribes would come to the trappers' rendezvous to trade, as well as to get in on the festivities. Tribes that were historical enemies to each other would temporarily put aside their differences at the rendezvous, since Ashley named it neutral territory. There would be no fighting in which blood was shed.

One particular tribe there that morning was the Arapaho Nation. Among them were members of the village of White Antelope, who camped two miles south of Sweet Lake. Among one particular lodge or tipi sat a beautiful twenty-year-old woman named Sweet Grass. She was a full-blooded Arapaho and daughter of the sub-chief, Two Hawks, and younger sister of Howling Wolf, one of the brave young warriors.

She was making breakfast, while her two-year-old daughter, Sara "Sunshine" Hancock, sat on a stump not far from her mother, playing with her doll. The little tot paused for a moment as she watched her mother make biscuits and eggs. Sitting not too far south from them was six-year-old Adam "Bear Claw" Hancock. He was making some new arrows for his bow that his uncle, Howling Wolf, made for him as a birthday present. His grandfather, Two Hawks, taught him how to make arrows. Even at such a young age, he was an adept student. When he wasn't wrestling with his friends, he would help his parents with chores or busy himself making arrows, since he was too young to own a gun.

Suddenly, the lodge flap opened, and out came the children's father, who was just waking up. His name was Azariah Hancock. Despite being just twenty-two years of age, he was a veteran of the fur trade. Coming out West eight years previously at the age of fourteen, he was a fugitive from Maryland. He met mountain man Liam O'Reilly in St. Louis, who took him under his wing and taught him everything about being a trapper and mountain man. Azariah would learn the trade from his mentor very well and became a successful trapper himself.

Now as he stood outside his lodge, he towered over just about everyone, because he was the tallest and largest man in the West, either white or red. Of English-Scottish ancestry, Azariah stood seven feet, five inches tall and weighed three hundred and fifty pounds, with almost no body fat whatsoever. As the white giant stood and stretched, his piercing blue eyes scanned the village, missing nothing, before falling upon the beautiful Arapaho maiden, Sweet Grass, who for the past seven years he proudly called his wife. Wearing long buckskin pants and completely shirtless, exposing his broad and barreled muscular chest, Azariah approached his loved ones. Sara (or Sunshine, as she is called by both names), squealed in delight as she ran to her father and held out her arms to be picked up. Without hesitation, Azariah bent down and took his little daughter in his huge sledgehammer-sized hands and picked her up, holding her high and smiling, exposing his even white teeth. Sara would giggle at her father and reach for his red hair that was braided Indian-style.

"Can we wrestle, Pa?" asked Adam as he stopped what he was doing and rushed over to his father.

Azariah was about to oblige his firstborn, but Sweet Grass momentarily intervened. "It is breakfast time," she said. "Now you and your father go wash up."

The little tyke frowned, but his father cheered him up. "After breakfast, we can wrestle," he said softly. "Maybe you can show your old man some new moves."

The boy's frown went immediately upside down as he and his father took his little sister down to the lake to take a bath. This was Azariah's favorite time of the day in which he would thank the Creator for waking him and his family to see another day, then thanking Him for his wife and two young children. While most men his age, particularly white men, would spend most of their young lives having fun in whiskey and women, Azariah was happy and content in raising his young family in the wilderness.

However, living in the wilderness was risky. As an adopted member of the Northern Arapaho Nation, Azariah knew that many of the tribe's enemies, such as the Crow, Ute, Pawnee, Shoshone and Blackfeet, were his enemies as well, but that is not what he feared. It was other trappers.

Early in his career, while under the tutelage of Liam O'Reilly, Azariah learned that trappers have more to fear from each other than they do from hostile Indians. According to Liam, at least Indians are honest about their feelings. If an Indian does not like you, nine times out of ten, you know it, but also if they believed that you are an honorable person and wished to be your friend, then you had a friend for life. Trappers who robbed other trappers for their plews would use deceit and racial ignorance as a weapon to prey on their victims. Both Azariah and his mentor, Liam, learned this early in their careers, which was why they trusted Indians more than they trusted their own kind, even hostile Indians.

Despite all this, both men were well respected among the trapping fraternity. Liam O'Reilly, who came out West back in 1806 at the age of sixteen, was a student of the legendary John Colter and an adopted member of the Northern Cheyenne, who were close allies of the Arapaho. At six feet, four inches tall, the thirty-eight-year-old Irishman was also a proven force to be reckoned with. Called Raging Bull by the tribes, he earned that name after avenging the brutal murder of his Cheyenne wife and infant daughter at the hands of a Crow war party thirteen years previously. Since then, he had had an ongoing feud with the Crow nation, but he has also had his fair share of battles with other trappers who threatened his life and the lives of his loved ones. Ten times out of ten, Liam always came out on top.

Azariah Hancock was just like his mentor, who he looked up to like a big brother. However, he surpassed even Liam O'Reilly in reputation, not just as a trapper, but as a feared and brave warrior. Given the name He Who Walks Tall by an Oglala Lakota medicine man when he first arrived in the wilderness, Azariah Hancock had earned a reputation of an honorable man, both among Indians and trappers alike. To his family and friends, he was a gentle, kind-hearted human being, who would put the safety of his adopted tribe first over his own happiness and desires. But it was his violent temper that had gained him such a positive reputation.

While marriages between trappers and Indian women were common during the fur trade, like most marriages of the time, they were not based on love. Even trappers who were seriously devoted to their Indian wives called them squaws and their children half-breeds. Azariah Hancock never called Sweet Grass that or any derogatory word, nor did he call his children half-breeds, nor would he tolerate anyone showing such disrespect towards his wife and children. Those who made that mistake paid with their lives as one poor trapper found out the hard way at the second annual Rendezvous two years prior.

At that Rendezvous, Azariah and Liam had just sold their plews and resupplied themselves for the next two seasons. Accompanied by Sweet Grass and Adam (who was then four years old and Sara was just a baby at three weeks old), the family was heading to the trading tents to buy some foofaraw. A group of highly intoxicated trappers blocked their path and one of them, who turned out to be the leader (and by the smell of his breath, the drunkest) had the nerve to demand that Azariah give Sweet Grass over to him and his friends for a couple of hours of fun in the bushes. The fact that the dumb son of a bitch called Sweet Grass a squaw was bad enough for

Azariah, but to think that the man thought she was a whore pushed him past the point of no return.

Azariah responded with a wicked right hook, knocking the drunk trapper unconscious before he even hit the ground. What happened next is still talked about to this day. While Liam, Sweet Grass, and a coalition of Cheyenne and Arapaho warriors who had just arrived to back them held the drunk trapper's friends at bay with rifles and bows and arrows, Azariah stood over the unconscious bastard, leaned down, and pried open his mouth, then reached into the man's mouth with one hand and ripped out his tongue with the strength of the Biblical character Samson or the Greek mythical character Hercules. Even Sweet Grass, who was more than grateful for her husband defending her honor, was shocked.

William Ashley, who just sold the Rocky Mountain Fur Company business to Jedediah Smith, David Jackson, and William Sublette was present, along with the new owners, as well as the legendary mountain man Hugh Glass, Jim Bridger, and black mountain man Jim Beckwourth, who could not believe what they just saw.

Ashley approached Azariah, demanding an explanation, but the twenty-year-old trapper was not in the mood to deal with the arrogant general's pompous bullcrap and was about to lay into him, while still holding the ripped tongue of the trapper. Fortunately, Liam O'Reilly and Jedediah Smith managed to intervene, and cooler heads prevailed. O'Reilly explained that the fallen trapper and his friends insulted Sweet Grass, and Azariah was forced to defend her honor as any loving husband would.

That was enough for everyone who heard the explanation, but Jedediah Smith had to ask, "Did you have to rip the man's tongue out?"

Azariah responded, "Any man who cannot control his tongue no longer has any use for it."

With that, Azariah threw the severed tongue at the feet of the drunken trapper's friends, who were sober enough to come to their senses and let him know there would be no more trouble from them. Azariah turned around, put his arm around his wife and infant daughter, and calmly walked back to their camp, with Adam and his Uncle Liam in tow.

As the crowd dispersed, Hugh Glass shook his head and said, "Now that was the damnedest thing I ever saw."

2

While Azariah was having breakfast with his family, his in-laws, led by Two Hawks, paid a visit. The children squealed in delight as they ran to their grandparents, who scooped up both kids to hug them.

"I hope we are not interrupting," said Two Hawks in the Arapaho tongue.

Azariah smiled at his father-in-law who was being pulled by the hand by little Adam. "You know you are always welcome at our table, Father," he answered.

Sweet Grass momentarily stopped what she was doing to welcome her parents and brother, Howling Wolf, with hugs and also quickly greeted her brother's wife, Prairie Bird Woman, and their three-year-old son, Little Badger. Clay Basket, who was the mother of Howling Wolf and Sweet

Grass, beamed with pride as she held Sunshine in her arms, while hugging her only daughter.

It had been a while since Azariah and Sweet Grass had seen their Arapaho family. During the two trapping seasons for the past seven years, they had lived in a cabin in a secluded valley in the Beartooth Mountains, along with Liam O'Reilly who lived three miles north of them. Despite that, they would visit their Arapaho relatives at least three or four times a year—before, during, and after Rendezvous—just so their children could get to know their kin. Even though Azariah and Sweet Grass were very happy, like most marriages of the time, it was far from easy. Earlier in their marriage, Sweet Grass found it strange and difficult to live far away from her people in a cabin all year round. The Arapaho, like most tribes, were nomadic; staying in one place for life was very foreign to them. Fortunately, Azariah was very accommodating and proposed to his bride to give it a try for at least a year. If she didn't like living in the mountains away from her kin, then they could live with them.

Now Sweet Grass was grateful for choosing to stay with her husband all this time. What made it even less strenuous was the fact that they, at Azariah's offer, would visit her family on more than two occasions every year.

"How is Raging Bull doing?" asked Howling Wolf. "He is usually here before you."

"He went to visit the Cheyenne," answered Azariah.

"Come to think of it, I am surprised that neither he nor anyone from Chief Black Cloud's village has arrived yet."

The statement got Two Hawks thinking as a worried look came upon Azariah's face. "It is probably nothing," said Two Hawks. "Raging Bull and the Cheyenne can take care of themselves, so whatever reason they are not here yet, I am sure it won't keep them away for long."

Azariah agreed with his father-in-law, but he was still concerned. "I hope you're right," said Azariah.

Sensing her husband's concern, Sweet Grass gently touched his hand to console him. "You shouldn't worry, husband," she said. "Raging Bull knows how to handle himself, especially if he feels his life is in danger."

Azariah smiled at her before giving her a peck on the cheek. It was at that moment, Otter Tail, one of Azariah's good friends, came over and announced that a band of Cheyenne had arrived at the Rendezvous. When Two Hawks asked if they were Black Cloud's village, he confirmed that it was and told Azariah that Liam sent him to let him know that he was on his way. By the tone of the message, Azariah sensed that it couldn't be good news.

The Irish mountain man arrived about a half an hour later to greet his friends and family, followed by his brother-in-law, Spotted Eagle, Spotted Eagle's son, Sparrow, and Chief Black Cloud.

"We were starting to get worried about you," said Azariah.

"Sorry for the tardiness, lad," said Liam. "But we have a good reason, and we also need to talk to you and Chief White Antelope and the Arapaho council."

"What is wrong, Raging Bull?" asked Two Hawks.

"We're putting together a rescue party, and we are hoping our Arapaho brothers will join us."

Azariah, Two Hawks, Howling Wolf, and Otter Tail showed surprised and questioning expressions on their faces. "Who was taken?" asked Howling Wolf.

"A couple of our women and children were taken in the middle of the night not far from here a couple of days ago," answered Spotted Eagle. "One of them was a widow and her two young daughters."

"Do you suspect who is responsible?" asked Azariah in the Cheyenne tongue.

"We followed their tracks towards here," said Liam. "Then they somehow turned southwest into Ute Country."

Azariah wasn't surprised, since he learned that the Utes would often kidnap women and children from enemy tribes and sell them to the Mexicans as slaves.

"There is something else, lad," said Liam. "We have reason to believe that white men are involved."

3

It had been almost a week since Bundy, his men, and their Ute allies snuck into the Cheyenne village and kidnapped a couple of Cheyenne women and children to add to their bounty. Among the new victims was Chokecherry Woman. She was a twenty-six-year-old widow, along with her two daughters, ten-year-old Bluebird and six-year-old Little Fawn. Chokecherry Woman's husband had been killed in a buffalo stampede the previous fall while he was hunting, and she had just completed her time of mourning when these Ute men jumped her and her two daughters by the lake that morning.

She was more afraid for her daughters and what these sick white bastards and their Ute allies had in store for them, but she managed to show no fear and tried to comfort her daughters and three other women from her village, by leading by example. When they stopped to camp for the night, Chokecherry Woman quickly noticed the three Blackfoot girls who were also captives. By their dress, she could tell that they were Kainai and that they were probably already abused by their captors. By the way one of the white men was looking at her and some of the other women, she could guess who did the abusing.

"What will happen to us, Mother?" asked Bluebird.

Despite that she was still bound behind her back, Chokecherry Woman managed to soothe and ease her daughter's fears. "Be strong, my child, not just for yourself, but for your sister as well."

"I hear Cheyenne women don't mess around until they get married," sneered Richard Dahmer.

"I have heard that too," said Charles Bundy. "Too bad these little ladies don't have a choice in the matter."

All the men, except for Gacy and Chapman, guffawed. The Utes weren't in a humorous mood either. Dahmer was about to approach Chokecherry Woman's daughters, but Red Knife and three of his warriors stood between them.

"No time for that," said Red Knife.

"Get out of my way, Ute," demanded Dahmer as he was about to go for his knife.

"You have already had your pleasure with the Blackfoot women," countered Red Knife. "Now is no time for anymore."

"Says who?"

Charles Bundy, sensing things were getting out of hand, gently put his hand on Dahmer's shoulder. "He is right, my friend," he said. "We need to get to Mexico as soon as possible and sell our very attractive merchandise."

"I am in no hurry," said Dahmer.

Bundy just smiled as he explained why they should be in a hurry. "You need to think more with your head than with your pecker," he said. "There is a strong possibility that a Cheyenne rescue party will be dodging our trail to try and get their women back."

"Don't forget those damned Blackfeet too," said Ted Gacy.

"Ted's right," added Boston Chapman. "I want to be halfway to Mexico by the time Buffalo Hump or any other war party catches up to us."

"Nobody is going to catch up to us," said Bundy. "We will camp tonight and continue tomorrow morning."

Sentries were set up to make sure none of the captives would escape and that no one would try to sneak upon them. Little did they know, both Buffalo Hump and the Kainai, as well as a coalition of Cheyenne and Arapaho rescue party led by Liam O'Reilly and Azariah Hancock, were hot on the villains' trail.

Liam, Azariah, along with Two Hawks, Night Wing, Howling Wolf, Otter Tail, Beaver and Chief White Antelope's grandson, Lone Wolf representing the Arapahos; and Spotted Eagle, his son, Sparrow, brothers Thunder Cloud and Pawnee Killer, along with their father, He Dog, brother-in-law Running Fox, Chief Black Cloud, Yellow Hawk (who was the father of Chokecherry Woman), and his son, Red Moon, representing the Cheyenne faction of the rescue party, immediately were on the hunt for their quarry.

Gideon, Azariah's faithful dog, now almost in his eighth year, picked up the scent of the kidnappers' trail. Everyone deduced they were heading to Ute country and then south. The dog may have been getting old, but his sense of smell had yet to diminish, and when he needed to be, he was a vicious killer. All his master had to do was say "sic 'em" and it was done.

While they were traveling, a plan was coming together on how they were going to get the Cheyenne women and children back from the kidnappers alive and unharmed. Everyone agreed that it would be foolish to go in half-cocked with guns blazing and turn an already dangerous situation into a worse one.

"I think it best that Raging Bull and I should spy on their camp once we have caught up to them," said Thunder Cloud. He was the oldest brother of Liam's late wife, Rain Cloud, and also the most skilled tracker in the group, with Liam being the second. No one disagreed.

There was no question of what was to be done with the

kidnappers once the rescue party caught up to them. Every-one knew Azariah would want to get first dibs on the ring-leaders, knowing his hatred for such despicable men. But first things first—catch up to them, try to get the women and chil-dren back without them being among the casualties, and then deliver true justice.

4

The coalition of Cheyenne and Arapahos were not the only rescue party hunting down the kidnappers. With Buffalo Hump and Kills The Enemy in the lead, the Blackfoot war party was also hot on the trail. The Blood war chief had decided that he would not rest until his daughters and his niece were returned and those responsible for their abduction pay for it to the highest degree. Kills The Enemy seconded that and swore on his life that he would search to the ends of the earth to bring back his daughter and two nieces. The young warrior, Dog Star, who had been courting Star Watcher, immediately volunteered to join the search party/war party to rescue and return the girls. Kills The Enemy graciously accepted, with no objection from Buffalo Hump.

Standing Bear, who was the best tracker in the group,

came upon what was left of the camp of the abductors. "The dogs we seek, four of them are riding horses that have iron shoes," he said. "I counted at least sixteen horses that do not wear such things."

Everyone knew that Standing Bear could tell by the tracks that the kidnappers who rode shod horses were white men and that they possibly had help from another tribe.

"What tribe would dare ally themselves with white men and kidnap our women?" said an angry Dog Star.

"It doesn't matter," responded Buffalo Hump. "They will all die a slow, painful death at our hands, once She Bear Woman, White Flower, and Star Watcher are safe."

The trail that Gideon had found led the rescue party to a small cul-de-sac near a cliff in the Uinta Mountains. It was clear to the rescue party that they were in Ute country and from what they found on the trail, the kidnappers were no longer in a hurry.

Liam O'Reilly deduced that the Indians who were helping the white kidnappers were Ute, enemies to both the Cheyenne and Arapahos. The dog led the Irishman and Thunder Cloud to the camp of the kidnappers. Keeping low, Liam took out his spyglass and saw the women they came to rescue. Chokecherry Woman and her two daughters, along with four other Cheyenne women. Then there were the three Blackfeet women who caught his attention. By their dress, or what was left of them, he could tell they were of the Blood tribe. He got a glimpse of the kidnappers and immediately recognized Charles Bundy and Richard Dahmer; the other two he didn't know.

"We have found them," he said in Cheyenne to Thunder Cloud.

"I will head back and bring the others," said Thunder Cloud. The Irishman just nodded.

Chokecherry Woman sensed that she was being watched and not just by these Ute dogs and their white masters. Someone was out there, and she sensed that someone was from the rescue party from her village. She already deduced what these four white men and their Ute dogs had in store for her, her daughters, their four friends from their village, and the three poor Blackfeet girls the men kidnapped since they were already in Ute country. She gave a silent prayer to Maheo that salvation would come and these dogs who kidnapped them would pay for what they have done.

"Thunder Cloud returns," said Pawnee Killer.

As soon as Thunder Cloud arrived in camp, he explained that they found their quarry. At that, Azariah and the men immediately packed up and rode out to Liam's position. It wouldn't be long before they got their women back and delivered justice to the bastards who kidnapped them.

5

Once the rescue party arrived, they formed up a plan, using sign language, so they didn't give away their position. It was decided that they would wait until nightfall, so they could have the element of surprise on their side. Azariah said a silent prayer to Jesus, asking to succeed and get the women back safely and that justice would be served.

The party split up. Azariah, Liam, Thunder Cloud, Beaver, and Gideon circled south of the cul-de-sac, where their quarry was camped. Azariah ordered Gideon to stay put, while they approached the camp. The rest of the rescue party circled north and east of the camp. Once everyone was in position, He Dog gave the sound of a hooting owl, to which Thunder Cloud responded in the same manner.

One of the Ute guards was suspicious of the owl calls, sensing that they didn't come from a bird of the night. Before he had the chance to investigate, Pawnee Killer let loose his arrow and it caught the Ute guard in the throat. The man was dead before he hit the ground. Another Ute was waking up to answer nature's call when he was set upon by Thunder Cloud. With his hand clamped shut over the Ute's mouth, the Cheyenne warrior sliced the man's throat from ear to ear. Azariah and Liam took down another guard, with Azariah breaking the man's neck like a twig. After that, the entire rescue party moved in. Chokecherry Woman was the first to see the men sneaking in and, despite the darkness, she recognized her father, Yellow Hawk, and brother, Red Moon. Bluebird and two of the women from their village were awake and were about to rise in excitement, but Chokecherry Woman immediately silenced them.

At that moment, Boston Chapman woke up to answer nature's call, only to be staring at Yellow Hawk as he was trying to release his daughter's bonds. Before he could react, Liam O'Reilly's rifle fired true, and the kidnapper's head exploded like a watermelon.

Suddenly, the camp exploded in excitement. Bundy and Dahmer tried to go for their weapons, but Dahmer was shot in the butt from Azariah's Hawken rifle, and Bundy was knocked unconscious from a Cheyenne war club, courtesy of Chief Black Cloud. Ted Gacy nearly escaped in the middle of the chaos, until he ran right into Gideon. That was the last thing he saw as the dog ripped out the white man's throat, blood splattering everywhere.

Yellow Hawk, Red Moon, He Dog, and Liam managed to get the women and children to safety, despite the arrows and musket balls flying all over the place. The Ute allies of Charles Bundy's party were being cut down left and right. Azariah cut down two warriors with his pistols and buried his Arapaho tomahawk in the skull of a third one. Otter Tail, Beaver, Spotted Eagle, and Lone Wolf were in hand-to-hand combat with some other enemy warriors, while the rest of the rescue party managed to take down the rest of the kidnappers.

When all was said and done, out of all the members of the kidnappers, only the ringleaders, Charles Bundy and Richard Dahmer, (despite that the latter was wounded in his back-side), were still alive. Red Knife was still alive but not for long. Otter Tail had cut open his stomach from side to side, exposing his guts all over the place. Two other Ute warriors were already being staked to the ground by Two Hawks and Howling Wolf and were being castrated. The rest of the villainous kidnapping party were dead.

The only thing left was the question of what to do with Charles Bundy and Richard Dahmer and the three Blackfoot women who were kidnapped.

"You go ahead and take the women back to the Rendezvous," said Azariah. "I am taking these three Blackfoot girls back to their people where they belong."

Everyone suddenly looked at Azariah like he'd lost his damn mind.

6

"You can't be serious," remarked Liam. "Do you have any idea what the Blackfeet will do to you?"

"I don't care," said Azariah. "These girls need to go back to their people, and I am also taking these two sick bastards with me and giving them over to the Blackfeet as a gift." Azariah pointed at Bundy and Dahmer and signed to the three Blackfoot girls to let them know he was taking them back to their people.

She Bear Woman wasn't sure if the giant white man was telling the truth or not, while White Flower and Star Watcher were downcast and didn't even pay much attention to him when he signed to them his intentions.

Realizing that the girls probably didn't believe him, Azariah took his Arkansas toothpick, cut their bonds free, and gave each of them an extra scalping knife as a gift that he always kept with his personals in his saddlebag. Once all three girls were free from their bonds and now armed, Azariah had their full attention and signed his intentions again.

This time, all three had a look of surprise on their faces, but She Bear Woman was convinced that this giant white man meant them no harm. She turned around and fully realized that the warriors who had claimed the lives of their kidnappers were Cheyenne and Arapaho and they had come to save the Cheyenne women and children. That still did not bode well for her and her sister and cousin, for the Cheyenne were among the many enemies of their people, so why was this white man who accompanied the Cheyenne, along with their Arapaho allies, so eager to help three Blackfoot girls?

White Flower and Star Watcher did not know what to make of the situation either, even after the giant had cut their bindings and given them scalping knives. They both sensed he had an ulterior motive.

Sensing their confusion and continued distrust, Azariah continued to sign to them to help ease their mind.

"Question," he signed. "What are you called?"

She Bear Woman spoke for all three of them. "I am She Bear Woman, and this is my sister White Flower," she signed. "We are Kainai and the daughters of Chief Buffalo Hump." She then pointed to Star Watcher. "This is Star Watcher, daughter of our father's brother."

Azariah smiled at all three women and signed to them

that they were safe now and were going back to their people. "I am called He Who Walks Tall of the Arapahos," he signed.

For the first time since their capture, a look of humor appeared on the girls' faces. It was Star Watcher who spoke in sign first. "You don't look like any Arapaho I have seen or heard of."

Azariah, along with some of his Arapaho and Cheyenne friends who were watching the exchange, laughed. "The Arapahos adopted me when I married one of their women," he signed in response. "I am known to almost all the tribes by my name."

"We have heard of you," said She Bear Woman.

A look of concern appeared on the faces of Liam O'Reilly, Two Hawks, and He Dog. They too were watching the exchanges and when they recognized the name of Buffalo Hump and Kills The Enemy of the Kainai, they knew that everyone who was not Blackfoot was being placed from the frying pan into the fire, even though they themselves had nothing to do with the girls' current predicament.

"If you have heard of me, then you know of my reputation," said Azariah in sign. "Then you would know that I speak with a straight tongue when I say I am taking you three back to your people where you belong, along with the two evil white men who took you against your will."

She Bear Woman and White Flower were convinced, but Star Watcher still had doubts. "Why would you do such a thing for us?" she asked. "You are an Arapaho by adoption, which makes you our enemy."

"I am also a white man, which makes me a double enemy to your people," said Azariah in both jest and seriousness.

She Bear Woman and White Flower giggled for the first time at the statement, but Star Watcher was still not convinced.

Azariah saw the look in her eyes, then he looked at Charles Bundy and Richard Dahmer. "Are these the two men who led this kidnapping party that took you against your will?" he asked the girls. "Did any of them rape you?"

The laughing stopped and the girls nodded and pointed at Richard Dahmer, who had the look of hatred in his eyes as he and Bundy were hogtied to a tree. Azariah could see that the hatred was towards him, which made him want to exact justice even more.

"Any man who forces himself upon a woman is my enemy," he signed to Star Watcher. "To me, it doesn't matter which tribe he is from or what the color of his skin is, a rapist is worse than a murderer, and I have no such mercy or sympathy for such men."

White Flower was not just convinced but a little impressed, while Star Watcher managed to ease up on her doubts. She Bear Woman was concerned whether her father and uncle would spare Azariah, even after what he did for them. She knew that, like most Blackfeet, they did not trust any white man, and they did not like what they did not trust.

She let Azariah know of her concerns, which raised the eyebrows of Liam, Two Hawks, He Dog, and even some of the other warriors who supported Azariah in his decision.

"Taking these girls back to their people I don't think is a good idea at this time, lad," said Liam. "Even though it is an honorable thing."

"I am not keeping them as my slaves," said Azariah in a risen tone that he did not mean.

"No one is saying you should," responded Liam. "But I have heard of Buffalo Hump and his brother, Kills The Enemy. Their reputations when it comes to us trappers is not exaggerated."

"What do you suggest?"

"Let's take them back to the Rendezvous, for now, get them cleaned up and something to eat, and then when they are ready, we can send them back to their people along with trade goods and some rifles as gifts."

"What about Bundy and Dahmer?"

"Kill the sick bastards. Justice has to be served for what they have done."

Azariah rarely questioned his mentor's logic, but what he said made sense. However, he had already promised to take these girls back to their people and give Bundy and Dahmer to their fathers to face justice. Azariah was always a man of his word.

As if reading his young friend's mind, Liam tried to convince him that he was not breaking his word. "The girls are going back to their people, alive and well. Sending them back better dressed, in better health and with gifts could easily diffuse an already tense and dangerous situation."

Azariah knew that Liam was only looking out for his best interests, but he didn't feel right in taking these girls farther away from their family and friends. Two Hawks, He Dog, and even Yellow Hawk came up with a solution.

Yellow Hawk approached the Blackfoot girls to speak to them. "As you know, He Who Walks Tall has every intention of returning you to your people," he signed. "But we fear for his safety as well. We know that your fathers are both mighty warriors and may kill He Who Walks Tall, despite what he has done for you three."

"My father and my uncle are both honorable men," signed She Bear Woman. "I give you my word that we will speak on He Who Walks Tall's behalf when he returns us to our people."

Yellow Hawk and He Dog were convinced, as was Azariah. "Is this good enough for you, Raging Bull?" asked He Dog.

Liam nodded.

"He Who Walks Tall should not do this alone," said Sparrow. "I will accompany you, brother, for I know these two white dogs will give you and these girls trouble."

"We are coming, as well," said Beaver, who along with Otter Tail had been long-time friends of Azariah since he had arrived among their people eight years previously. Sparrow had long considered Azariah a brother since he saved his life from an angry buffalo during a surround so many years ago. Even Howling Wolf, Azariah's brother-in-law, volunteered.

The white giant was grateful for his friends' services, but he was concerned that he might be putting them in danger. "You do me honor, but I don't know what will happen once we reach Blackfoot country," said Azariah. "I believe these girls will speak on our behalf to Buffalo Hump and Kills The Enemy, but I doubt many of their warriors will have any qualms in taking our scalps once the girls are safe."

"We cannot and will not let you do this by yourself, He Who Walks Tall," said Howling Wolf. "My sister will never forgive me if I allowed you to turn her into a widow."

"I love Sweet Grass more than life itself, my brother," responded Azariah. "But what good will it do her if she loses both a husband and a brother? Who will look after your children and mine?"

"Do not ask us not to accompany you on this dangerous journey, my brother," said Beaver. "As long as I have known you, you have put your life on the line for so many, not just my people, but for people you barely knew, even at the risk of your own happiness."

Azariah turned red at his friend's praise of him. What Beaver said was no exaggeration, since Azariah was considered one of the most unselfish and bravest men that anyone had ever known or met, despite that even at twenty-two years of age, Azariah wasn't the kind of person who sought or enjoyed praises of himself.

"I do these things, Beaver, because it is the right thing to do," he said. "I am just a man, no different than any other."

"To us, you are more than that," said Sparrow. "You are our friend and our brother. That makes you family, and families look after each other."

"Which is why we are coming with you," said Howling Wolf. "If you ask us not to come with you, then you are asking too much."

Azariah knew he could not dissuade his brother-in-law and his friends from joining him. He noticed Otter Tail was quiet. "I notice you haven't said anything, my friend."

"Because you don't even need to ask me," answered Otter Tail. "I am of the same opinion as everyone else. Besides, I do not trust the Blackfeet, despite what those women say."

"Then it is settled."

7

Meanwhile, about fifty miles north in Cheyenne country, Buffalo Hump and Kills The Enemy, along with their rescue party, had their own issues.

"It appears that our quarry has doubled back and headed into Ute country," said Standing Bear. He was the best tracker in the rescue party, but he did not want to inform his chief and his brother that he was losing the trail. Even though the tracks led them into Cheyenne country southeast of their village, it was true that whoever had taken She Bear Woman, Star Watcher, and White Flower were crafty and had doubled-back and gone into Ute country, and the trail was fading.

"It doesn't matter where the trail leads!" shouted an angry Kills The Enemy. "I will go to the ends of the earth to find my daughter and kill those who took her from me and her mother."

"I stand with you, Kills The Enemy," seconded Dog Star.

Buffalo Hump was just as angry and concerned for his own two daughters as well as his niece, and he wanted nothing more than to get his hands on those who kidnapped them, but he was more sensible and had more patience and wisdom in situations such as these. He could also tell that Standing Bear wasn't telling the whole story about the trail they were following by the look of concern on his face.

"There is something you are not telling us," he remarked to the tracker.

Standing Bear refused to lie to his chief or to Kills The Enemy, for that matter. He had great respect for them both and had been on many hunts with them and many battles. "The trail is fading," he said. "As I mentioned earlier, whoever took your daughters is crafty, and all I can tell you is that it leads into Ute country."

"The Ute country is where we shall go and get our daughters back," said Buffalo Hump.

"And deliver justice to those who dared to take them from us," added Kill The Enemy.

Little did the Blackfoot rescue party know, but She Bear Woman, Star Watcher, and White Flower were returning to them safe and sound, escorted by Azariah Hancock and his Arapaho and Cheyenne friends.

Azariah and his party left the main camp to head north

the next morning. She Bear Woman was in the lead, for she knew that the land of her people was north of their current location. Azariah had never traveled into Blackfoot country, mainly because he never had any reason to before. Despite living deep in the Beartooth Mountains, which was Crow country, Azariah was one of the very few trappers who never had any run-ins with the dreaded Blackfeet.

Liam O'Reilly had taught him well over the years that the Blackfeet considered the beaver sacred and resented the trappers encroaching on their land to hunt and trap the 'flat tail,' as they called the beaver.

Despite his fearsome reputation and his temper, Azariah was a man of peace and never went looking for trouble. Even though the Blackfeet were a nomadic tribe and went wherever they pleased, Azariah believed that any trapper who deliberately went into Blackfoot country was looking and asking for major double trouble.

As he and Howling Wolf were keeping an eye on their two prisoners, Beaver and Sparrow struck up a conversation, through sign language, with Star Watcher and White Flower. The girls were grateful that they were going home and the two ringleaders who were responsible for their ordeal were going to be punished, but they were still surprised that warriors from an enemy tribe were willing to risk their lives to get them back to their people. Sparrow explained that it was all He Who Walks Tall's idea and that they had him to thank.

"I have never met a man like him before," signed White

Flower. "My father, Buffalo Hump, is the most compassionate and courageous man that I know, but I never thought I would meet his equal, especially a white man."

The young Cheyenne warrior laughed. Just two years younger than Azariah, he remembered the day he and Azariah became lifelong friends. "He Who Walks Tall saved my life many years ago when we were just boys," he signed. "Even among my people, men like him are of rare quality."

"Why is it important to him that these two white men who took us against our will receive punishment?" asked Star Watcher. "He doesn't even know us or owe us anything."

"He could have kept us as his slaves if he wanted," added White Flower.

"He could have," said Beaver. "But that is not the kind of man he is, and he despises men who take women against their will."

"Why is that?" asked White Flower.

Beaver and Sparrow looked at each other and shrugged. "You will have to ask him," they both signed.

The Arapaho and Cheyenne warriors knew why, but they felt they did not have the right to answer that question. Only their friend and brother, He Who Walks Tall, had that right.

———

Meanwhile, Liam O'Reilly and the Cheyenne and Arapaho rescue party were on their way back to the Rendezvous with their rescued women and children. They decided to camp not far from the river to give the women and children time to rest, relax, and recover from their ordeal. Night Wing and Lone Wolf went hunting for game, while Two Hawks got the fire started. Red Moon went to take the horses out to graze, while the rest of the remaining rescue party stood guard. Liam was extremely worried about Azariah and those who went with him to return the Blackfoot women back to their people. He admired his best friend and pupil for doing the right and honorable thing by those women, but he was afraid for him and Howling Wolf, Beaver, Otter Tail, and Sparrow. The three Blackfoot girls he trusted, but their people, especially their fathers, was another matter. Liam thought it best to take the girls back to Rendezvous and send them on their way later with gifts for their families. But he and Azariah didn't always see eye to eye when it came to doing the right thing.

He was brought out of his reverie when he saw Yellow Hawk talk to his daughter and granddaughters. Chokecherry Woman and the girls had just come in from bathing and were gathering more firewood when Night Wing and Lone Wolf came back with a yearling elk over one of the packhorses. The women immediately went to skinning and gutting the animal for their dinner. By the time they were done, Red Moon had the horses staked out and came in just as the meat was cooking on a spit.

Few words were spoken as everyone filled their bellies. Bluebird and Little Fawn were exhausted and immediately went to sleep after their mother tucked them in for the night. Liam, He Dog, Red Moon, Two Hawks, Pawnee Killer, and Spotted Eagle volunteered to stand guard, while everyone slept. Later that night, wolves howled as the full moon reached its zenith. The howling woke up Little Fawn who had a healthy fear of wolves. Chokecherry Woman tried to comfort her youngest daughter, who couldn't stop crying out of fear.

"There, there, my child," said Chokecherry Woman. "The wolves are only singing to the moon. They cannot hurt you."

"I am afraid, Mother," responded Little Fawn. "They're coming to eat us!"

"I won't let anything happen to you or your mother and sister, little one," said Liam, who had been listening from a distance. "Your mother is right. The wolves are just singing to the moon, but if even they think of coming anywhere near us, your grandfather, uncle and I will make them pay."

"You promise, Raging Bull?" asked Little Fawn as she wiped the tears from her eyes.

"On my honor, I will not let anything happen to you or your mother and sister." Liam then turned to Chokecherry Woman and asked, "May I sing for your daughters? From my experience, singing usually calms the soul of a child."

Chokecherry Woman granted her permission, and the

Irishman sang a tune from his childhood that his mother used to sing. It had the intended effect, and within seconds Little Fawn was back asleep in her mother's arms. Chokecherry Woman whispered a thank you to Liam, who just bowed his head in response before going back to guard duty.

In the darkness, he could feel He Dog, Pawnee Killer, Spotted Eagle, Two Hawks, and even Yellow Hawk who was awake, smiling at him.

8

Azariah and his party were on the move the next morning. This time Azariah's dog, Gideon, jogged beside She Bear Woman's horse in the lead, followed by White Flower and Star Watcher. Azariah on top of his giant Appaloosa stallion rode behind them, with Howling Wolf riding beside him, and Beaver, Otter Tail, and Sparrow watching their backtrail with the evil prisoners, Charles Bundy and Richard Dahmer, riding between them, bent over their horses.

The two scums of the earth would not remain quiet during the night, despite being bound and gagged, and they rankled the men, especially Azariah. The wound on Dahmer's right butt cheek was getting infected, not that it mattered. He knew he was a dead man, whether it would be at the hands of the Blackfeet or Azariah Hancock, but he wasn't going out without a fight.

Charles Bundy was a different story. He didn't want to die and tried to shame Azariah for turning in two fellow white men to the Blackfeet over a group of squaws. Under normal circumstances, Azariah would have already killed the two kidnappers and rapists. But he did not want to rob the Blackfeet of the pleasure of delivering justice for their daughters, which is why he gagged the two bastards instead. Now, they were grating on his last nerve, and he called a halt.

He got off his horse and walked back to the two men. After he removed Dahmer's gag, the doomed rapist spat at him and shouted obscenities about his mother and Sweet Grass. Azariah responded by cold-cocking Dahmer with a right hook, knocking him unconscious. He did the same to Bundy and all was well as he returned to his horse with all three Blackfoot women and his friends, smiling.

At that moment, Gideon growled as he was staring north of their position. Azariah immediately saw the cause of his dog's attention—from north came a whole war party of Blackfeet, and they were heading straight for them.

———

Sweet Grass had woken up in a cold sweat. Something was wrong. She often did that when Azariah was away, either hunting, trapping, or on a rescue mission as he was on now with Liam. She was not surprised that her husband volunteered to go with the rescue party to help their Cheyenne friends bring back their women and children who were kidnapped. That was the kind of man her husband was.

As a child, she had always been a good judge of character, but she never thought she would marry a white man, especially one she had happily spent the last seven years of her life with and raised two healthy beautiful children. Like many among her people, Sweet Grass had heard the stories of white men taking red women as their wives for a season or two and then abandoning them and their children to return back East to the land of the whites. Some of these men had wives and children back East that the red women didn't even know about. However, for some reason, Sweet Grass had a sixth sense that Azariah was not like any of those men, and she was grateful that she was right. He was an excellent husband and a devoted father to their two children, and she felt she knew him better than anyone else.

But it wasn't always like that. Earlier in their marriage, she found it strange that instead of living with her people all year round, he suggested that they move deep to a valley in the Beartooth Mountains, which was home of their enemy, the Crow. Even when she saw the cabin that Azariah had built, with the help of Liam, she at first could not understand why her husband wanted them to stay in a wood lodge for the rest of their lives. She thought her husband was truly strange, but now she was grateful he had them move to the cabin because it was better to stay in a lodge where you did not have to worry about heat escaping from the inside during the winter and was a strong and impenetrable force against enemy and animal attacks. With a tipi, you would constantly have to keep the fire going to keep the heat up during the cold nights, especially during the winter, and they were not made to stay in one place, since the Arapaho, like most tribes of the Northern Plains were nomadic.

However, with Azariah's promise that they would visit their Arapaho family at least three or four times a year, it made the transition even better. Sweet Grass had no regrets. Even during the tough times, she and her husband were a team. There were no secrets between them, especially about Azariah's past. Sweet Grass understood her husband's hatred toward rapists after what happened to his twin sister. It was clear to her that he never fully recovered from that, even though he avenged his sister's rape. Many nights Azariah woke up screaming out his sister's name, crying and unable to sleep, and Sweet Grass was there to comfort him, stroking his red hair as he laid his huge head on her lap and she would sing him back to sleep. This what brought them close as husband and wife, and even though the nightmares were now gone, the anxiety and depression that Azariah went through were still there.

For Sweet Grass, Azariah was more than just her husband, partner, and protector. They were soulmates. Not long after they were married, Azariah told her about the Lakota medicine man, High Cloud, who saw him in a vision and told him that the Great Spirit had chosen a path and if he chose to walk that path, then a woman would walk it with him. That is when she knew that they were meant to be together forever.

Sweet Grass often thought about Azariah's family back East. He spoke highly of his parents and sister, and she often wondered what it would be like to meet them. She definitely would have liked their children to get to know their father's family; however, Azariah rarely spoke about his family since the birth of their daughter. Sweet Grass thought might be because of what happened to his sister, Abigail, but despite this, she prayed that one day if the Man Above willed it, she would meet her husband's family.

Right now, her husband's whereabouts was her concern. Did he and Liam, along with the rescue party, catch the kidnappers and deliver justice? She prayed that all was well and everyone was safe and wherever Azariah was, he was not only safe but would return to her and their children.

———

"You're blowing everything out of proportion," said Liam O'Reilly in annoyance to Pawnee Killer.

"Am I, brother?" said Pawnee Killer. "Everyone sees how Chokecherry Woman looks at you and how you blush when she does."

The rescue party had been on the trail back to Rendezvous for the past couple of days and would arrive in another day or two. Liam was getting annoyed because He Dog, Thunder Cloud, and Pawnee Killer were teasing him about keeping company with Chokecherry Woman and her daughters. Liam was more worried about Azariah and the boys, and the fact he could not do anything about that situation ate at his craw.

After singing Little Fawn to sleep that night, the girl had asked to ride with the Irishman, with her mother's permission, of course. While they rode, Liam and Chokecherry Woman had been in a conversation mostly about his concern for his young friend and pupil. But his father and brothers-in-law saw something between the two and thought now was the time to have a heart-to-heart chat.

"Raging Bull, how long has it been?" asked He Dog.

"How long has what been?" responded Liam.

"You know what I am talking about. I know you loved my daughter very much, but even she would not want you to mourn her for the rest of your life."

"And you think Chokecherry Woman would replace her?" said Liam.

"Of course not," said the Cheyenne elder. "No one can replace my daughter, but I and many of your brothers believe it is not good that you should be alone for the rest of your life."

"Father is right, Raging Bull," said Thunder Cloud. "You are a good man, and a good man should never spend the rest of his life alone."

"Agreed," added Pawnee Killer. "I mean, what kind of life is that for any good man without a good woman to share it with?"

Spotted Eagle, Running Fox and Black Cloud had been listening. "Black Cloud and I have been talking with Red Moon," said Spotted Eagle. "He and his father believe Chokecherry Woman would welcome you as a husband."

"And Bluebird and Little Fawn would welcome you as a father," added Chief Black Cloud. "Maheo knows they need one after losing their own father."

Liam had heard how Chokecherry Woman's husband lost his life a year previously on a buffalo surround. It was not surprising, because that was the most dangerous way to hunt buffalo. Her husband, Soaring Hawk, was a good man and a doting father to his two daughters. His death left a huge emptiness in his family, just like the death of Rain Cloud and Constance left a huge emptiness in Liam's life. He did enjoy Chokecherry Woman's company and that of her daughters, and he was never against the possibility of getting married again; he just did not want to lose another person he loved dearly.

He envied Azariah and Sweet Grass for that. Despite the odds, they survived the past seven years and counting, and even at such a young age, Liam was proud of how mature the young, happily married couple was and how well of a job they were doing in raising their young children. Even though Liam was not related to Azariah, he was honored that the

Hancock children, Adam Bear Claw and Sara Sunshine, called him uncle, but he still longed to have a family of his own again.

Maybe what his father- and brothers-in-law were trying to tell him made sense. More importantly, what if the Creator Maheo was giving him another chance at having a family? Liam was not a religious man. He believed in God, but he did have questions, especially with his Irish Catholic upbringing. However, one thing he knew for sure, that everyone kept harping on—Rain Cloud would not want him to mourn her the rest of his natural life. She would want him to move on, and Maheo seemed to be giving him that opportunity.

"Does Yellow Hawk and Red Moon approve of a possible courtship between me and Chokecherry Woman?"

He Dog smirked. "Approve of it? They're encouraging it!"

———

She Bear Woman, White Flower, and Star Watcher asked Azariah and the men to let them do the talking when the Blackfoot war party coming toward them surrounded them. As they got closer, the girls automatically recognized their fathers, Buffalo Hump and Kills The Enemy, from a distance and immediately rode out to greet them.

The Kainai war chief and his brother immediately called a halt as they saw their daughters and jumped off their horses to greet them. It was a tearful reunion as Buffalo Hump held his two daughters in his arms and Kills The Enemy held his daughter in his. After what appeared to be an eternity, She Bear Woman freed herself from her father's hug for a moment to explain about their ordeal and quickly introduce the Cheyenne and Arapaho warriors who not only helped free them but volunteered to return them to their people. They were led by a giant, red-headed white man named He Who Walks Tall.

Suddenly the eyebrows of not only Buffalo Hump and Kills The Enemy raised up, but so did those of every Kainai warrior in the rescue party.

"I have heard of this giant white man who lives among the Arapaho," said Buffalo Hump. "You said he and a group of Cheyenne and Arapaho warriors saved you and brought you back to us?"

"Yes, Father," answered She Bear Woman. "They killed the Ute warriors and all but two of the white men who kidnapped us."

"I was just about to ask who took you girls from us," said Kills The Enemy.

"Father," said Star Watcher. "He Who Walk Tall brings the two leaders of the men who kidnapped us as a gift, so they can face punishment for what they have done."

"Does he now?" said Kills The Enemy.

He and Buffalo Hump looked at each other as if they read each other's thoughts. They could not believe that an enemy, especially a white man, would risk his life to return three Blackfoot women to their people, along with the surviving men who kidnapped them to face justice. Not that they did not believe their daughters; but the brothers as well as the rest of the rescue party had to see this for themselves.

"Let us go and meet this strange white man and his Arapaho and Cheyenne brothers," said Buffalo Hump. The girls got back on their horses and led their fathers and warriors back to where their saviors were.

As the girls returned with their people, Azariah, Howling Wolf, Beaver, Otter Tail, and Sparrow all had nervous looks on their faces, along with their two doomed prisoners, as the Blackfoot war party surrounded them. She Bear Woman, White Flower, and Star Watcher sat on their horses between their fathers and Azariah who stared at Chief Buffalo Hump and Kills The Enemy.

Gideon growled at the Blackfoot warriors but was quickly silenced by his master. "Easy, boy," said Azariah.

Howling Wolf, who brought his horse up next to his brother-in-law's, had his rifle ready just in case they needed to get out of there in a hurry. "Moment of truth, brother," he said.

Azariah just nodded in agreement.

9

"I am He Who Walks Tall of the Arapahos," signed Azariah. "We return your daughters to you and bring the men who took them from you to face justice."

At first, Chief Buffalo Hump sized Azariah up and down and concluded that, one, this giant white man could probably challenge his whole war party in hand-to-hand combat and was hard to kill; and two, that there was something about him that showed he was a man of honor. Something about his demeanor, his eyes, and his whole body manner told the feared Kainai chief that this white man at least was no enemy; and if he were, he was one who would deserve an honorable death. The chief prayed that he was not wrong. Everyone was waiting on his response as he was thinking this.

"You're taller than you should be, He Who Walks Tall," he signed.

At that, everyone except one of the Kainai warriors snickered and laughed. That warrior was looking at Azariah long, hard, and cold. Some of the warriors were hoping to take some scalps, especially from an enemy with strong medicine and such a well-deserved reputation, but Buffalo Hump was the leader of this party, and they trusted his judgment and respected his decision-making.

"I can't help how the Creator made me," responded Azariah. "But I have no complaints or regrets."

At that moment, Azariah slowly turned and signaled Beaver, Otter Tail, and Sparrow to bring Charles Bundy and Richard Dahmer, who was still knocked out from his punches. "The bastards who took your daughters," he signed. "The one with the hole in his butt raped all three of them."

Buffalo Hump, Kills The Enemy, and Dog Star frowned at the two prisoners. It was clear their fate was sealed, but what was going to happen to Azariah and his friends?

"We offer you their lives for what they have done," signed Azariah.

Kills The Enemy, though grateful, was not impressed. "What makes you think that we won't take your life and those of your friends along with these dogs?"

"Father no," pleaded Star Watcher. "It would be wrong to kill them after what they did for us!"

"Be quiet, girl," responded Kills The Enemy. "You don't make decisions here!"

Howling Wolf gripped his Hawken rifle tightly. Beaver

and Otter Tail clearly were nervous and slowly moved to cock their rifles, while Sparrow and Azariah both looked to be calm. Gideon was on the verge of growling again, but Azariah silenced him with a gesture of his hand.

"You must be Kills The Enemy," signed Azariah.

The Kainai warrior and elder nodded.

"Your daughter and your brother's daughters are very brave and strong women. You both should be proud of them."

"They told us what you and your brothers did for them and for that we are grateful," said Kills The Enemy. "My question is why?"

"Good question," said Buffalo Hump. "You and your warriors have already rescued your Cheyenne women that these white dogs and their Ute allies took along with our women. You could have kept them yourself."

"Because that is not who I am," answered Azariah. "I don't believe in slavery, and any man who rapes a woman is not human and is an enemy without honor."

The Kainai warrior who stared at Azariah with a cold look smirked. "Maybe you are an enemy without honor," he signed. "Or maybe you are a woman yourself."

Azariah had noticed this man's attention on him earlier and automatically decided he did not like him.

"That is Stomp The Snake," said Buffalo Hump. "He is a warrior who doesn't know his place when his leaders are speaking."

Stomp The Snake went quiet but continued to give

Azariah the cold look. The giant trapper turned his attention back to Buffalo Hump and Kills The Enemy.

"I wish to answer your earlier question, Kills The Enemy," he signed. "I personally have no quarrel with the Kainai or your friends the Siksika, Pikuni, and Atsina, and I have heard of both your fearsome reputations from my adopted tribe, the Arapahos, and our allies the Cheyenne. Your daughters speak very highly of you both, especially about your reputation of being men of honor."

Buffalo Hump raised an eyebrow to his two daughters, who were smiling, but had their heads down. "Where is the honor in killing the men who not only saved your daughters but brought them back of our own free will, even when some of our closest friends advised against it?"

"I assume you believe that we are no longer enemies, hey?" asked Kills The Enemy.

"I am under no assumptions," said Azariah. "I know that the Blackfeet hate trappers and rarely show mercy to an enemy, so if you must kill me, I ask two things."

"They are?" asked Buffalo Hump.

"Spare the lives of my brothers," answered Azariah. "Allow them to return to their families."

Howling Wolf, Beaver, Sparrow, and Otter Tail all objected.

"I am not going back to face my sister and explain to her why she is a widow and why Bear Claw and Sunshine no longer have a father!" shouted Howling Wolf in the Arapaho tongue.

Sparrow signed, "I am a Cheyenne warrior. We do not abandon our brothers and friends in the face of death or leave them to the enemy. If you are asking me to do that, He Who Walks Tall, then you are asking too much!"

Beaver and Otter Tail seconded that and signed that they would not abandon their white brother, especially to the Blackfeet.

"Then you will all die today," signed Stomp The Snake.

Azariah had had just about enough of the arrogant jackass. "You first, Stomp The Snake," he signed. "Today is a good day to die!"

"Enough!" shouted Buffalo Hump in Blackfoot and in sign. He then turned to Stomp The Snake and said, "I decide who lives and who dies today, not you!"

There were a few men that Stomp The Snake was afraid of. His chief and Kills The Enemy were among those few.

"No one will die today," said Chief Buffalo Hump, "until we get back to our village. You had a second request, He Who Walks Tall."

Azariah pointed at Bundy and Dahmer who was just coming to. "I wish to see justice done," he said. "I want to see these two bastards die!"

———

Liam O'Reilly and the rescue party returned to the Arapaho village of White Antelope and the Cheyenne village of his friend Black Cloud that were both camped at Rendezvous. Chokecherry Woman and the girls, along with the rest of the Cheyenne women and children who were kidnapped by Charles Bundy and his minions, were reunited with family and friends. Sweet Grass and her mother, Clay Basket, along with Howling Wolf's wife, Prairie Bird Woman, had gotten wind of their return and headed toward the Cheyenne village with their children. When they got there and found that neither Azariah nor Howling Wolf was with the returning rescue party, they sensed something was terribly wrong.

Liam and Two Hawks immediately went to greet them and quickly explained about the three Blackfoot women who were among the kidnapped, along with the Cheyenne women, and that Azariah volunteered to return them to their people. Two Hawks explained that Howling Wolf, Beaver, and Otter Tail, along with the young Cheyenne warrior, Sparrow, volunteered to go with him. The women were the opposite of happy.

"You let our son and our daughter's husband go on a foolish mission into Blackfoot country?" shouted Clay Basket at her husband.

"It was He Who Walks Tall's idea," said Two Hawks. "Raging Bull tried his best to convince him otherwise not to do this, even though it is the honorable thing to do."

"That honorable thing is going to turn our daughters into widows," snapped Clay Basket.

Sweet Grass managed to remain calm. She was still not happy that her husband and brother were headed into Blackfoot country, but she was not surprised. Her husband was known for risking his life to help others, especially innocent people he barely knew. It was one of the things she loved about him, but it also terrified her. She was scared for him.

"I am sure there was nothing anyone could have done, Mother," she said. "Raging Bull and father would have had a better chance of roping the wind."

"You could say something like that," said Liam. "Ladies, I swear, if the boys are not back within a week, I will personally go find them."

"I will go with Raging Bull also," said Spotted Eagle who had been listening. "My son Sparrow is with your husband, and I am worried about his safety as well."

"It will take a week for them to get to Blackfoot country and back," said Liam. "Assuming those girls were able to convince their fathers not to kill He Who Walks Tall, Howling Wolf, Sparrow, Beaver and Otter Tail."

"And just who are the fathers of those three Blackfoot girls?" asked Clay Basket.

Liam gulped. "Chief Buffalo Hump of the Blood Nation and his brother, Kills The Enemy."

Clay Basket fainted, Prairie Bird Woman went berserk, and Sweet Grass just shouted, "Creator help us!"

10

Azariah and his friends rode with Buffalo Hump's party back to their village, after the chief smoked the peace pipe with them at the insistence of his daughters and niece. Nearly all the members of Buffalo Hump's party were surprised that the white giant known as He Who Walks Tall wanted to see the men that kidnapped their women get punished, Blackfoot-style. Howling Wolf, Beaver, Sparrow, and Otter Tail knew the method behind their white brother's madness. They respected him for it, but Howling Wolf was a little concerned for his brother-in-law. Azariah had killed many men for the crime of rape over the past years, as long as anyone from both the Arapaho and Cheyenne Nations had known him. While skin color didn't matter to him, the rapists that Azariah Hancock had sent straight to hell had been other white men. That didn't mean he never killed an Indian, but he never killed one in cold blood or for the crime of rape. Azariah could count the number of Indians he had killed on one hand, and all of them were in self-defense or battle. But Howling Wolf felt that despite Azariah's heart being in the right place, he felt his sense of justice was a dangerous obsession. He wasn't alone in that department. Sweet Grass had been concerned for her husband for quite some time. While she never told anyone about it, Howling Wolf knew his sister better than anyone and felt he needed to talk to his brother-in-law.

"May I have a word with you, brother?" he asked Azariah in Arapaho.

Azariah nodded and signaled his brother-in-law up to ride next to him. The two had always been close, even before they became family.

"Do you trust Buffalo Hump and Kills The Enemy?"

"We smoked the peace pipe," answered Azariah.

"That is not what I asked," said Howling Wolf with a raised eyebrow.

Azariah shrugged. "I believe they are honorable men, so yes, I do trust them."

"What about the rest of them?" asked Howling Wolf, nodding over at Stomp the Snake who was ahead of the train, riding with Blue Duck.

"Stomp The Snake seems to have a problem with me, but I doubt that is what you wanted to chat with me about."

"I am worried about you, brother," confessed Howling Wolf.

Azariah smiled. "You and your sister both."

"What you're doing is honorable, but your obsession with men like Bundy and Dahmer and wanting to see them dead... well, it scares me and Sweet Grass, as well," said Howling Wolf.

"I never thought I would give you or your sister reason to fear me," responded Azariah.

Howling Wolf smirked. "We're not afraid *of* you, but *for* you."

The young trapper sighed. He knew his actions, no matter how honorable and justified they were, would cause concern among those he cared about. "You of all people know why I do what I do."

"The bastards who raped your sister and Wandering Bear's granddaughter are dead," said Howling Wolf. "You made sure of that, and you can't go on punishing yourself for situations you had no control over."

"This is not about me punishing myself for what happened," said Azariah.

"Stop lying to yourself," responded Howling Wolf. "This is me you are talking to."

"Then you know this is bigger than me or those I love." The young warrior gave his brother-in-law a surprised look. "I could not protect my sister, nor could I have prevented what happened to Wandering Bear's granddaughter," said Azariah. "No innocent woman, or child for that matter, should ever suffer the way they suffered. If I can't stop something like that from happening, then I will avenge it and make those who inflict such suffering upon the innocent pay dearly with their lives."

"To do that, brother, you must stop being human and become a spirit," said Howling Wolf.

Buffalo Hump, Kills The Enemy, and the girls were riding not that far ahead and were pretending not to hear the conversation between He Who Walks Tall and Howling Wolf, but the Kainai chief was curious about what was being said, even though he could not understand the Arapaho language in which the conversation was being spoken.

At that moment, Dog Star rode up to the family, next to Kills The Enemy and Star Watcher. "It makes my heart glad to see that you and your cousins are safe."

Star Watcher smiled at the young warrior who had been attempting to court her for quite some time.

Her father for the first time looked approvingly at him as a sign of acceptance. "I have been meaning to ask you," he said towards Kills The Enemy and Buffalo Hump. "What is your opinion of He Who Walks Tall?"

"Now that is an interesting question," said Buffalo Hump.

Kills The Enemy just shrugged. "He has proven to be an honorable man, but he is still a white man."

"You don't trust him, Father?" asked Star Watcher.

"What do you think, daughter?"

"He did save our daughters' lives, brother," said Buffalo Hump. "Knowing that they were Blackfeet and at the risk of his own life and the lives of those who followed him."

"Don't forget, he even brought the two ringleaders of those who kidnapped us to face justice, Uncle," said She Bear Woman.

"I am not blind, my niece," said Kills The Enemy "But just because certain snakes are not poisonous does not mean they are harmless, for a snake is still a snake and they can still bite."

"And that is how you see He Who Walks Tall?" asked She Bear Woman.

"That is how I see all my enemies, especially whites," answered Kills The Enemy.

To a point, Dog Star agreed with the man, who he hoped would one day be his father-in-law. Certain snakes were not poisonous but can still bite, but he wasn't sure He Who Walks Tall was among those enemies who should be compared to a snake. "I have heard stories about He Who Walks Tall, and if any of them are true, then I must respectfully disagree with you, Kills The Enemy."

Suddenly the eyes of Kills The Enemy, Buffalo Hump, She Bear Woman, White Flower, and a smiling Star Watcher were on the young Kainai warrior.

"And just what stories have you heard, Dog Star?" asked Buffalo Hump.

The young warrior looked over his shoulder at the giant trapper and his brother-in-law, who were still in conversation, before he returned his attention back to his chief to answer his question. "I heard that four summers ago, he and his Arapaho brothers killed eight French trappers who kidnapped two Nez Perce girls."

"How did that happen?" asked a surprised Kills The Enemy.

"I was told that they were out hunting when they stumbled upon the French trapping party, who were in the middle of raping the two girls," answered Dog Star. "He Who Walks Tall became enraged at the sight of two girls being violated like that and immediately started killing the trappers one by one."

The girls gasped in amazement, while their fathers remained expressionless as Dog Star continued the story.

"Of course, he had help from his Arapaho brothers, but not one trapper escaped; in fact, three survived, only for He Who Walks Tall to stake them to the ground, spread-eagled, and cut off each of their manhoods and then managed to skin all three of them alive for what they had done."

"What happened to the Nez Perce girls?" asked White Flower.

"He Who Walks Tall returned them to their people along with the heads of the French trappers that he didn't skin," answered Dog Star.

"How do you know this?" asked Buffalo Hump.

"You know my uncle, Ten Bears, who lives among the Pikuni?" The chief nodded. "One of his three wives is a Nez Perce woman that he captured two summers ago," answered Dog Star. "Cutting Off Heads Woman is her name, and she told me the story when I went to visit them last winter. It just so happens that one of the two girls that was taken is her cousin."

It was at the moment a commotion erupted from the back and everyone turned their attention to the cause. One of the villains, Charles Bundy, managed to break free from his bonds and was making a break for it.

11

_____

For a moment, everyone just watched as the former kidnapper-turned-prisoner made his escape on foot.

"Does that idiot actually believe he is going to get away from us on foot?" said Buffalo Hump.

"What color is he, brother?" laughed Kills The Enemy as he prepared to catch the escaped prisoner. "I will bring him back. I could use some amusement."

"Wait, brother," said Buffalo Hump. "Look."

Everyone except Howling Wolf, Beaver, Otter Tail, and Sparrow looked surprised as Azariah, on top of his large Appaloosa stallion, rode after Bundy. In less than a split second, he caught up to him and with one open hand slapped the back of the villain's head, knocking him off balance in mid-stride and causing him to fall face first into the ground. By the time Bundy was struggling to get back to his feet, Azariah was on him, knocking him back down to the ground.

"You did not think you going to get away that easily?"

The villain was outraged and had a look of pure hatred that Azariah had seen many times before from his enemies. "Piss on you!" he shouted as he spat in the giant's face.

Azariah calmly took out one of his bandanas from his pocket to wipe the spit off his face. Then without warning, in a swift motion, he took his Arkansas toothpick from his belt and sliced off Charles Bundy's right ear. The villain howled in pain as shouts of approval came from the rescue party of Buffalo Hump. The Kainai chief himself was immediately impressed with Azariah's actions. To add insult to injury, Gideon trotted up to Bundy, lifted one of his hind legs, and as his master held Bundy down, urinated on where the man's right ear used to be. This brought huge laughter from everyone except Stomp the Snake who still gave Azariah and his coalition of Arapaho and Cheyenne brethren a look of hatred and distrust. Dick Dahmer who was still bound and bent over his own horse, was too weak from the now-infected bullet wound in his backside to even look up.

———

At the village of Black Cloud near the Rendezvous, things had quieted down since the rescue party's return. A feast and dance were held in the honor of the men who successfully rescued the kidnapped women and children. Around the same time, it was immediately decided among both the Arapaho and Cheyenne councils of White Antelope and Black Cloud that if He Who Walks Tall and those who volunteered to go with him in returning the three Blackfoot girls to their people did not return within a week or two, a second rescue party and possible revenge party would go into Blackfoot country to find them.

Despite the festivities, Liam O'Reilly was concerned for his longtime partner and friend. He knew Azariah could take care of himself and had learned everything he had been taught about the ways of the mountain man, but even the best still go under. The Irishman shared Sweet Grass's concern about her husband's sense of honor. Going into Blackfoot country, even just to return three kidnapped Blackfeet women to their people, was suicide. While Liam personally did not have any grudges or feuds with the Blackfeet, like most trappers, he did have his fair share of run-ins with them.

While in thought, a twig snapped behind him, and he quickly turned to see Chokecherry Woman smiling at him. He doffed his wolverine skin cap and gave a slight bow, along with a slight gentle smile to the young Cheyenne widow. "Not many people can sneak up on me like that," he said in the Cheyenne tongue.

"I didn't mean to bother you, Raging Bull," said Chokecherry Woman "I wanted to thank you for what you did for me and my daughters."

The Irishman blushed a little but refused to take full credit. "Your father and brother were there too," he said. "It wasn't just me alone."

"True, but they didn't manage to successfully calm my daughter, Little Fawn, of her fear of wolves by singing her a lullaby," responded Chokecherry Woman.

Liam laughed. "You speak with a straight tongue. How are Bluebird and Little Fawn?"

"They are well, thanks to you," answered Chokecherry Woman. "And how are you this evening?"

Liam just shrugged. Chokecherry Woman could tell he had a lot on his mind since they returned. "You are worried about your friend, He Who Walks Tall?"

Liam just nodded. "What he is doing is honorable, but still I have trust issues when it comes to the Blackfeet."

"It is in the hands of Maheo," said Chokecherry Woman. "He Who Walks Tall and those who went with him to return those girls to their people will return unharmed."

"I wish I had your confidence," said Liam. "Maybe Sweet Grass, Prairie Bird Woman, and Clay Basket will reconsider attempting to scratch my eyes out."

Chokecherry Woman laughed. "Sweet Grass, is she He Who Walks Tall's wife?"

"She is," answered Liam. "She is the best thing to ever happen to him."

"And you?"

"What about me?"

"Don't you have a wife?"

A look of sadness came upon Liam's face. Chokecherry Woman realized she may have hit the wrong button and quickly apologized, but Liam just shrugged. "I had a wife and a daughter," he said. "Crow killed them."

"I am sorry for your loss," said Chokecherry Woman.

"It was a long time ago and they were avenged."

Changing the subject, Chokecherry Woman's next question surprised Liam. "Will you come and say goodnight to my daughters?" she asked. "Little Fawn would love for you to sing to her again."

Liam gave a smile and said, "Lead the way.

12

As Buffalo Hump's party arrived at the village, the reunion between She Bear Woman, White Flower, Star Watcher, and their mothers was bittersweet. Bundy and Dahmer were immediately taken and staked to the ground, spread-eagled, while all the attention was on Azariah, Howling Wolf, Beaver, Otter Tail, and Sparrow. Gideon stayed close to his master's side and growled at anyone not familiar to him who tried to get close. Azariah, Howling Wolf and Sparrow had slightly nervous looks on their faces, while Beaver and Otter Tail were stoic and put up a brave front as the five friends stood in the middle of the Kainai crowd in the village of Buffalo Hump.

The chief and his brother, Kills The Enemy, along with Dog Star and Standing Bear stood between the council, the rest of the crowd, and Azariah and his friends as the girls explained to their mothers and their people how these men, led by the giant white man called He Who Walks Tall, saved them from captivity by the bad white men and their Ute allies. She Bear Woman announced that it was He Who Walks Tall who volunteered to return her and her sisters back to their people and brought the two ringleaders who were responsible for their abduction to face justice.

There was a mixture of gasps of amazement and surprises on the faces of many in the Kainai crowd, including elders of the council and many Kainai warriors, veterans of battles with enemies of the people who have heard of this giant white trapper that lives among their enemies, the Arapaho. Some shared Kills the Enemy's distrust and hatred of all white men, even though they also agreed with the fact that what He Who Walks Tall and his friends did was honorable and appreciated. Most believed because of that alone, the white trapper and his friends should be released and allowed to return to their homes, while others, like Stomp The Snake, wanted to scalp and torture these men regardless of the honorable deed.

Stomp The Snake most definitely wanted Azariah's scalp, believing that taking the life of such an enemy with strong medicine was big medicine itself. Both Buffalo Hump and Kills The Enemy suspected Stomp The Snake's intentions, but they knew he wouldn't defy them or the council, since it was agreed that the council would decide what would happen to He Who Walks Tall and his friends.

While Kills The Enemy didn't fully trust the white trapper, he did appreciate what he and his brothers did in saving the life of his daughter and nieces and assured them that he along with his brother would speak on their behalf to the council in letting them live and allowing them to return to their people.

After the girls were done, Buffalo Hump spoke. "I stand with my daughters and niece and believe that He Who Walks Tall and his brothers have done an honorable thing for us, and it would be wrong to take their lives. That being said, I believe that we should let them live and allow them to return to their home among the Arapaho and Cheyenne." Buffalo Hump used sign language as he spoke for the benefit of Azariah and his friends.

It was at that moment an elderly man stepped out of the crowd and spoke. "In saving the lives of our women and returning them to us, along with the two ringleaders who were responsible for their abduction, it is good and appreciated; however, it does not change the fact that one of them is a white man, adopted by the Arapaho, three of them are Arapaho themselves, and one is Cheyenne. That alone makes them our enemy."

Dog Star signed to Azariah, saying, "That is Red Shield. He is our medicine man." Azariah and the rest nodded.

Red Shield turned to Kills The Enemy. "Tell me, Kills The Enemy, do you share your brother's opinion?"

Kills The Enemy turned to the quintet in question, then

to his brother, and finally his two nieces and daughter. "Everyone here knows my mind," he said, "but I believe these men, though our enemies, have done an honorable thing, so yes, I believe it would be right and honorable to let them go."

Many among the crowd, as well as those among the council, nodded in agreement, but Stomp The Snake was not going to let this issue rest without his voice being heard. "Are we Kainai or are we weak-willed women?" he shouted. "This white man is our enemy, so are the Arapaho and the Cheyenne. Letting them go because of one good deed sets a bad precedent."

"Stomps The Snake speaks the truth," added Blue Duck. "Think of what not only our enemies the Crow, Nez Perce, Assiniboine, and Flathead will say about us, but our allies, the Atsina, Pikuni and Siksika."

Many in the crowd nodded, despite that most were for letting Azariah and his friends go. Red Shield turned to Azariah and signed, "What say you, He Who Walks Tall?"

Azariah turned to his friends as if asking for their permission to speak on their behalf. They nodded back to him before he gave the Kainai holy man his response. "Stomps The Snake speaks with a straight tongue." The response shocked Stomps The Snake. "We are your enemies, now, today, tomorrow, and maybe forever," said Azariah. "But even enemies can show each other respect."

Buffalo Hump, Kills The Enemy, Dog Star, Red Shield,

and even Blue Duck nodded in approval of Azariah's response. Stomps The Snake was unimpressed and frowned.

"We shall have a council and decide what will happen," said Red Shield.

"Since my brother and I have spoken on behalf of He Who Walks Tall and his friends, it is only fair that they should stay with me and my family," said Buffalo Hump.

No one disagreed, and Azariah and Howling Wolf both signed their thanks to the chief. However, the trapper nor his friends took their eyes off Stomps The Snake, who continued to stare coldly, mostly at Azariah. This did not go unnoticed by Buffalo Hump and Kills The Enemy and they assured Azariah and his friends that they were safe in the village until the council had made their decision. Kills The Enemy secretly warned the quintet not to turn their backs on the young Kainai warrior. It was a piece of advice greatly needed and heeded, for Stomps The Snake was going to do whatever he wanted, no matter what the council's decision.

13

Back at the Rendezvous in the village of White Antelope, Sweet Grass and the children were getting restless. "Mama, when is Dada coming home?" asked little Sunshine. She missed her father very much, as did Bear Claw. "When are going to see Pa again?"

Sweet Grass smiled at her children and tried to be strong for them. "Your father will return to us, my little ones," she said. "Do not fear."

It was at that moment Grandfather Two Hawks and Grandmother Clay Basket arrived along with Prairie Bird Woman and her three-year-old son, Little Badger. Sweet Grass turned to her father with hopeful eyes, if he had any news on her husband and brother.

Two Hawks did his best to both console and reassure her and his daughter-in-law. "Nothing new as of yet, but do not fear, my daughters," he said. "He Who Walks Tall and Howling Wolf are brave and trained warriors. We have not come this far to lose them now."

Sweet Grass and Prairie Bird Woman said nothing but put up a brave front for their children's sake. "I wonder how Beaver and Otter Tail's families are handling this?" said Clay Basket.

"I spoke to Wandering Bear," said Two Hawks. "They are just as concerned as we are, but it is the hands of the Man Above."

"My father will return!" shouted Bear Claw.

All the adults looked at the young six-year-old who puffed out his chest and stood, showing a brave front. "If he doesn't then I will go find him and make those who took him from us pay!"

Two Hawks and Clay Basket smiled and laughed, while Sweet Grass, though surprised, showed a sign of pride at her son. "What gives you such confidence that your father will return?" she asked.

"Because he is the mighty He Who Walks Tall, and he is with my uncle, the mighty Howling Wolf," answered Bear Claw. "Together they can beat anybody!"

Two Hawks beamed with pride at his eldest grandson. The women were just glad to have a little ease of tension in the room and a break from worry. There was some truth in the boys' boasting, though, Sweet Grass thought. For as long as she had known her husband, Azariah Hancock had never lost a fight. Whether it was a regular fistfight with other trappers or a shootout with hostile warriors from enemy tribes or rogue trappers, her man always came out on top. The same thing could be said for her brother, Howling Wolf, and even Liam O'Reilly as well.

Sweet Grass had witnessed first-hand the number of times her husband put his life on the line to protect their family, friends, and even total strangers who were nothing more than innocent bystanders, and she loved him for it. She considered him the most unselfish man she had ever known, other than her father and brother, which made the marriage even stronger. Azariah had a strong relationship with his in-laws, and if he considered Liam O'Reilly the big brother he never had, then Howling Wolf was the twin brother he never had. This is why Sweet Grass was not surprised when her husband volunteered to take the three Blackfoot captives back to their people and her brother volunteered to go with him. They were always thinking of others and not themselves.

She remembered what Azariah told him of his parents' teachings from their God about "Doing unto others as they would do unto you." His parents... that was the first time in a long time Sweet Grass thought of them. Her husband's family, whom she longed to see, whom she owed her happiness to. Abigail, his beloved twin sister whose honor he defended after a vicious man violated her. Then being forced to flee after killing that man. Sweet Grass couldn't understand why her husband was forced to flee his family after avenging the brutal rape of his sister. Even after he explained the white man's laws to her on many occasions, it made little sense. Azariah did what any loving brother or a decent man would have done. Either way, she was grateful to the Man Above for this giant, strange, but loving and unselfish white man she married.

Before she even met Azariah, never in her young life did she ever dream of marrying a white man. Even after he told her the story about the Lakota medicine man, High Cloud, about the path the Great Mystery had chosen for them both, she never thought this would happen. Now she prayed that she would not lose him, especially to the feared Blackfeet. She needed him, the children needed him, and she hoped that the Man Above would bring him and her brother back safe into her arms.

———

Back at the village of Buffalo Hump, as the council was in discussion about what was to be done with Azariah and his friends, the former was in deep thought. Thinking of Sweet Grass and the children, Azariah prayed that the Kainai council would show mercy and allow him and his friends to return home to their families. Azariah Hancock feared no man. He had a healthy fear of animals, like the grizzly bear, but it was a controlled fear. While he had many battles with hostile Indians such as the Ute, Crow, sometimes the Shoshone, mainly because they were enemies to the Arapaho and Cheyenne, he was one of the few trappers who had either little or almost no encounters with any member of the Blackfoot Confederacy and their allies. Mainly because he, like Liam, made it a point to avoid trapping in their territory, not out of fear of getting killed, but out of respect.

Liam and Azariah were among of the few trappers who knew that the beaver was sacred to the Blackfeet and that was at least one of the many reasons the tribe was so hostile to all white men, with a few exceptions. The trappers from the Hudson Bay Fur Company from Canada, for example, did have an uneasy trade agreement with the Blackfeet. "Treat and respect people the way you would want to be treated and respected," Azariah's father always said. His father? This was the first time in a couple of years that he thought of his father or any of his family back in Maryland. *Damn*, thought Azariah. *Has it been eight years already?*

Azariah had been haunted about what happened to his beloved twin sister, Abigail. Even though he avenged her rape and sent Belshazzar Jones to hell for what he did to her, it had always been hard for him to sleep at night, because he was in constant worry not knowing how his sister and parents were doing. He was also ravaged by guilt in the feeling that he failed to protect his sister, which for a while caused him to have nightmares and wake up in a cold sweat.

Sweet Grass cured him of that. She was truly the best thing to ever happen to him. He now believed at least they were meant to be together. Many nights she would sing to him to calm him when he would have bad dreams or when he was in a bad mood. When their daughter was born, the nightmares ceased. Azariah was grateful to God for his wife and children and his in-laws and friends, as well, which was why he prayed that his life and that of his friends who came with him did not end today in a Blackfoot village. He prayed that the council would do the right and honorable thing and not be swayed by the hotheads like Stomps The Snake. Azariah was still trying to figure that man out, when Buffalo Hump returned to the lodge.

"The council will see you now, He Who Walks Tall," said the chief.

Azariah, Howling Wolf, and their friends had been staying with the chief and his family. Little Bird was a gracious hostess as were She Bear Woman and White Flower. The latter struck up a conversation through sign language with the young Cheyenne warrior, Sparrow, asking him if he had a woman. While her mother strongly disapproved, her older sister giggled, while Azariah, Howling Wolf, Beaver, and Otter Tail were grinning at him from ear to ear when the chief returned. Azariah signed a thank you to Little Bird for an excellent dinner and for her kindness as he and the others were about to stand and leave before Buffalo Hump held up his hand.

"Just you, He Who Walks Tall," signed the chief.

A look of concern came upon the face of the trapper. "And what of my brothers?" he signed.

"They are still under my protection," answered Buffalo Hump. "Do not fear for them. No harm will come to them or you, for that matter."

That was good enough for Howling Wolf and the others who encouraged Azariah to go with the chief. With that assurance, Azariah nodded and followed Buffalo Hump to the council, hoping he was not making a huge mistake that would cost him his life and the lives of his brothers.

14

Chief Buffalo Hump led Azariah through the village to the council lodge. As they were walking through, the trapper noticed Charles Bundy and Richard "Dick" Dahmer still staked out in the ground. Both were still alive but in pain. The bullet hole in Dahmer's backside had been infected for some time now, so he was a dead man either way. Bundy was still crying over his missing right ear and cursed Azariah Hancock for his current predicament.

"Will I at least get to see those two tortured to death?" asked Azariah in sign.

Chief Buffalo Hump smiled and signed, "That is one of the things we wish to speak to you about. Come."

They continued to a very large tipi in the center of the village. The lodge flap was open, and Buffalo Hump went in first and Azariah followed. Gideon, who always followed his master, was ordered to stay outside of the council lodge.

As they entered the council lodge, Azariah noticed that the entire group was in a circle. It was a mixture of elders and warriors. Most of the warriors appeared to be men in their late twenties to early fifties, and they sat in line next to the elders, while the much younger warriors sat behind them. Azariah noticed Stomps The Snake among the older warriors, and he appeared the opposite of happy. He continued to give the giant trapper a cold, hard stare, but Azariah ignored him as he followed Chief Buffalo Hump to an empty spot near the back center of the council circle. Carefully not breaking any courtesy taboo when it came to seating arrangements, Azariah followed Buffalo Hump's instructions as the chief pointed him to sit next to Kills The Enemy. As he sat down, his eyes missed nothing, and noticed that most of the men, except for Stomps The Snake and those who followed him, were stoic and showed little expression. Dog Star, who sat among the younger warriors, at least gave Azariah a slight smile and a nod, which Azariah returned.

With everyone in place, all attention was on the giant. Chief Buffalo Hump was the first to speak using sign language for Azariah's benefit. "The council has decided because of what you and your friends have done in rescuing and returning our women, along with the two leaders who kidnapped them, that we should let you go."

Azariah was relieved and nodded his thanks, but the chief

was not done.

"You requested that you wish to see these two white men, who kidnapped my daughters and my niece, to suffer," he signed. "Why?"

"From what your daughters have told me, one of the men raped them," answered Azariah. "I hate rapists with a passion. Any man who forces himself on any woman is not a man at all, he is not even worthy to be called a coward, for that would mean he is human."

A slight scoff came from Stomps The Snake, which Azariah noticed, but ignored.

"You have had some experience with such men before?" asked Red Shield.

Azariah nodded and answered, "I have seen the pain and suffering such men have inflicted on the innocent, and it is an act that is hateful to me and unforgivable."

"Is that why you killed those French trappers four summers ago near the Bitterroot Mountains?" asked Dog Star.

A shocked look appeared on Azariah's face as the council members who were surprised at such a revelation began to mutter amongst themselves. When everyone quieted down, Azariah asked, "How can you possibly know that?"

"So it is true?" asked Kills The Enemy.

The trapper nodded his affirmation of the story. Dog Star explained to Azariah that one of his uncle's wives is Nez Perce and is a cousin of one of the two Nez Perce girls.

15

_____

Back at the village of Black Cloud near the Rendezvous, Liam
O'Reilly was checking on his horse when he got a surprise
visitor.

"Greetings, Raging Bull," said Yellow Hawk as he walked
up behind the Irishman, taking him off guard.

"Not many people can sneak on me like that," said Liam.
"I must be losing a step in my old age."

"Waugh," said the Cheyenne Elder. "I am much older
than you and will surely leave this world for the Happy
Hunting Grounds before you and my children."

"I pray that does not come anytime soon," said Liam.
"How are Chokecherry Woman and the girls doing?"

Yellow Hawk sighed in relief and smiled before answering, "Better, now that they are home, thanks to you."

"It wasn't just me," said Liam. "We had plenty of help from He Who Walks Tall and our Arapaho friends."

"This is true," said Yellow Hawk as he patted down Liam's horse. "Do you worry about your young friend?"

"I do, but I taught him well, so I know he can handle himself."

"What about the Blackfeet?" asked Yellow Hawk. "Do you trust them to be honorable and not kill He Who Walks Tall and those that went with him after what he did for them?"

"Good question," said Liam. "I can only pray to Maheo that Chief Buffalo Hump will spare their lives after they rescued and returned his daughters to him."

"What does Spotted Eagle say?" asked Yellow Hawk. "His son, Sparrow, went with He Who Walks Tall to return those Blackfoot girls to their people."

"We have talked, and he is as worried as I am," said Liam. "But he has heard of Buffalo Hump and believes that he is an honorable man, even though he is an enemy."

"I too have heard of Buffalo Hump and his brother, Kills The Enemy," said Yellow Hawk. "But they are not the only men of honor that I have heard." Liam raised an eyebrow at that statement. "I hear that He Who Walks Tall has quite the reputation of being an honorable man himself."

The Irishman laughed. "It is not something he encourages, but yes, he has a well-earned reputation of making the most difficult, but honorable decisions."

"You sound very proud of him," said Yellow Hawk.

"He Who Walks Tall is like a younger brother to me," said Liam. "I am very proud of the man he has become."

"Then he must have learned from the best," said Yellow Hawk.

Liam O'Reilly sensed that there was a reason the Cheyenne elder was speaking to him, after just paying him a compliment. "I never considered myself an honorable man, Yellow Hawk," he said. "I just do what I have to."

The elder smiled. "Which is why I want to speak to you about my daughter."

So there it is, Liam thought. "I am not just grateful for what you have done for Chokecherry Woman and my granddaughters," said Yellow Hawk. "As you know, she is a widow and has been for over a year now."

"You think I am a worthy man to be her husband?" said Liam.

"I don't think it, I know it," said Yellow Hawk. "She would welcome you as a husband, and Bluebird and Little Fawn would welcome you as a father."

Liam just sighed, but as if reading his thoughts, the Cheyenne elder continued. "I know about your wife and child, Raging Bull, and what the Crow did to them. I know you miss them very much, as much as my daughter misses her husband and my granddaughters miss their father."

"I don't have any right to take his place," said Liam.

94

"That is for them to decide," countered Yellow Hawk. "You both have been alone too long."

"Did He Dog put you up to this?" asked a suspicious Liam.

The elder just grinned.

"I thought so."

"Talk to my daughter," said Yellow Hawk. "What can it hurt?"

I guess it can't, thought Liam.

———

Later that day, Liam went to the Arapaho camp to check on Sweet Grass and the children, who along with Two Hawks, Clay Basket, and Prairie Bird Woman were worried sick about Azariah and Howling Wolf.

"Uncle Liam!" shouted Adam as he ran to greet the Irishman. He was followed by his baby sister, Sara, and their cousin, Little Badger, as they all ran up and grabbed their uncle by both legs.

Liam scooped up all three giddy tots into his big arms as he was greeted by their mothers and grandparents, who had just exited their lodge. He could see the concerned look on their faces, which begged the unasked question.

"Welcome, Raging Bull," said Two Hawks. "Any word yet on He Who Walks Tall and Howling Wolf?"

"Not yet."

Sweet Grass' expression said it all. Liam tried to reassure her and Prairie Bird Woman. "Do not lose hope. Your husbands can take care of themselves, and they have Beaver, Otter Tail, and Sparrow with them."

"I know Azariah can take care of himself, Liam," said Sweet Grass. "Still doesn't mean I cannot worry about him. I love him too much."

Liam just smiled as he handed Sara back to her mother. "Why did you let them go, Raging Bull?" asked Prairie Bird Woman in the Arapaho tongue.

Before Liam could answer, Clay Basket spoke up. "What could he have done?" she said. "When Howling Wolf and He Who Walks Tall make a decision, no matter how difficult it is, if it is the right decision, you have a better chance of roping the wind."

"Well said, wife," said Two Hawks.

"I didn't want them to go," said Liam, speaking in Arapaho. "I tried to convince He Who Walks Tall that taking the three Blackfoot girls back to their people was not a good idea, but you know how he is. Howling Wolf, Beaver, Otter Tail, and Sparrow just went along with him."

"This Buffalo Hump," said Sweet Grass, "do you believe he will spare their lives and let them return to us?"

"I cannot be sure," said Liam. "His daughters and niece promised us that they would speak on He Who Walks Tall's behalf, but will that be enough?"

"If he is an honorable man, it should," said Two Hawks.

"I wish I had your confidence," said Clay Basket.

Like Liam and Yellow Hawk, Two Hawks did not know the Blackfoot war chief Buffalo Hump personally, but he knew of his reputation and that of his brother. He knew they were ruthless and merciless when it came to their enemies, but if their daughters said that no harm would come to his son and son-in-law after saving them and returning them to their people, well, that was good enough for the Arapaho elder. Trying to convince his wife, daughter and daughter-in-law of that was the problem.

"Why don't you come in, Raging Bull? We were just about to eat."

"Thank you," said Liam. "Other than coming to check up on ya'll, I could also use some advice."

"What kind of advice do you need?" asked Two Hawks.

The Irishman gave a slight grin. "Marriage."

Everyone eyes lit up as they sat down for dinner.

"Oh," said Clay Basket. "Who caught your eye?"

"More like me being caught by her," laughed Liam. "Her name is Chokecherry Woman."

"Yellow Hawk's daughter?" asked Two Hawks.

Liam nodded. The women had a questionable looks on their faces, but Two Hawks explained that Chokecherry Woman and her two young daughters were among the rescued captives. "She is a widow," said Liam. "Her husband was killed during a buffalo surround last summer."

"Have you spoken with her?" asked Sweet Grass.

"We have talked since we got back. She is a fine woman."

"What does her father say?" asked Two Hawks.

"Same thing that everyone in Black Cloud's village is saying," answered Liam and left it at that.

Two Hawks just grinned, while the women giggled.

"You have been without a woman for a long time, Raging Bull," said Clay Basket. "What does your heart say?"

Liam was quiet for a moment. "To be honest with you, I don't know," he said. "It's not that I don't want to get married again..."

"You're afraid of losing another loved one," said Sweet Grass.

"I swear you and your husband are made for each other," said Liam in mock anger. "You both read minds."

"A trait she shares with her mother," said Two Hawks with a smile.

"Go to her and tell her how you feel, Raging Bull," said Clay Basket. "You're not the only one who has lost someone dear to you."

"And be truthful," added Two Hawks. "Women love it when you speak with a straight tongue. You will live longer."

Clay Basket punched her husband in the arm, while everyone laughed. Liam thanked them for the helpful advice and filed it in the back of his head.

16

"You are an interesting man, He Who Walks Tall," said Red Shield. "Tell me, how many of our people have you killed?"

Azariah, who just overcame his initial shock about how the Blackfeet heard he rescued two Nez Perce girls, was in thought for a moment. "I speak in a straight tongue when I say I have never killed a Blackfoot, warrior or otherwise," he signed.

Some on the council were skeptical, but Azariah continued to explain. "I have never traveled into the country of your people or your allies, nor have I had any run-ins with you anywhere else."

"Interesting," said Red Shield. "Trappers come into our territory to trap the flat tail all the time," said Chief Buffalo Hump. "How come you don't?"

Azariah just smiled. "You can say out of respect, for I am

told that the flat tail is sacred to you," he signed. "And I happen to enjoy living without being reckless."

Some of the elders, including Kills The Enemy, laughed. Buffalo Hump just grinned and shook his head, but Stomp The Snake continued to remain silent and stare coldly at the trapper.

"He Who Walks Tall, you mentioned that you have seen and experienced the pain and suffering that men like those who took Buffalo Hump and Kills The Enemy's daughters have caused," signed Red Shield. "When did this happened to you?"

Azariah was silent for a moment. He could feel every eye on him, which made him uncomfortable again. However, he saw no reason to lie or keep his pain a secret from this council. "Not me," he signed. "It was done to someone that I loved dearly, my twin sister."

The council was quiet for a moment until Dog Star spoke. "That explains a lot," he said.

"So you act out of vengeance?" asked Buffalo Hump in sign.

Azariah just shook his head. "I had my vengeance and got justice for my sister," he answered. "I kill rapists because no woman should ever have to suffer the way she did. No man has the right to force himself on a woman or take her against her will."

"Says who?" asked Stomp The Snake. "You white men

have been doing that to our women as long as I can remember."

"The white men are not the only ones who are guilty, Stomp The Snake," said Red Shield. "I am sure our enemies the Crow, Flatheads, Nez Perce and Cree are appreciative every time you visit their women during a raid."

"What's your point, old man?" snarled Stomp The Snake.

"His point is you're no different than the white men you hate, who have harmed our women," said an angry Buffalo Hump. "Now be quiet and show some respect."

"I have no respect for my enemies," responded Stomp The Snake. "Especially my white enemies, and you are all fools in deciding to let this white dog and his friends live!!"

Azariah had had enough. "You want my scalp, Stomp The Snake?" he signed. "You are welcome to try and take it anytime."

The arrogant Kainai warrior stood in defiance and drew his knife. "I will not just take your scalp, white dog, but I will pay your Arapaho bitch a visit and show her what a real warrior is!"

That did it. One second, Azariah was sitting between Chief Buffalo Hump and Kills The Enemy; the next second, he launched up at Stomp The Snake, grabbing him by the throat with one hand and wrenching his knife arm with the other. It took the entire council to pull the two men apart. Three men held down Stomp The Snake, while six men were having trouble just trying to calm Azariah and keep him from turning the whole scene into a massacre.

Stomps The Snake was no small man. At five feet, eleven inches and a muscular one hundred and seventy-five pounds, he was a force in his own right. But despite the fact that he never lost a fight in hand-to-hand combat, he was clearly no match for Azariah, who dwarfed him by almost two feet and outweighed him by one hundred and seventy-five pounds of solid muscle. Surprisingly, that did little to intimidate or frighten the Kainai warrior.

"I fear nothing, white man!" shouted Stomps The Snake in Blackfoot.

Dog Star translated for Azariah, who managed to calm himself but not by much.

"I have killed better men than you and grizzly bears that were bigger, taller and much stronger than you," added Stomps The Snake. "I challenge you to a fight to the death!"

"I gladly accept," responded Azariah after the challenge was translated.

Buffalo Hump and Kills The Enemy just shook their heads in disbelief. They weren't angry at Azariah for accepting Stomps The Snake's challenge. The warrior had insulted Azariah's wife, and their guest had every right to defend her honor. They were angry because Stomps The Snake was a fool and they told him as much. The trapper could tear him into a million pieces with his bare hands alone, but the stubborn warrior would not be swayed.

"Since you issued the challenge, Stomps The Snake," signed Azariah, "you can pick the weapons."

The arrogant warrior retrieved his knife with one hand and then grabbed his war club with other. The latter had a sharp metal spike at the end of it. "Will this do?" asked Stomps The Snake.

Azariah responded by taking out his Arkansas toothpick and his Arapaho tomahawk, which was specially made for a man his size. With the challenge accepted, it was agreed that the fight would take place in the center of the village.

Howling Wolf, Beaver, Sparrow, and Otter Tail, along with Buffalo Hump's family, were just leaving the chief's lodge in response to the commotion. Gideon was barking up a storm, when Azariah and the council had exited the council lodge and were moving to the center of the village. Charles Bundy and Richard Dahmer, who were still staked to the ground, were all but forgotten as word spread through the entire Kainai village about the impending fight between Stomps The Snake and the white trapper known as He Who Walks Tall.

Howling Wolf, Beaver, Otter Tail and Sparrow were allowed through the crowd led by Gideon, as they walked up to Chief Buffalo Hump and Kills The Enemy.

"What is going on?" asked Howling Wolf through sign language.

"Stomps The Snake has challenged He Who Walk Tall to a fight to the death," answered Buffalo Hump.

Howling Wolf was shocked but not entirely. Stomps The Snake had been itching for a fight since the rescue, and it was only a matter of time. The Arapaho warrior was surprised that his brother-in-law would accept such a challenge. "What did Stomps The Snake do for He Who Walks Tall to accept his challenge?"

It was Dog Star who answered. "He insulted He Who Walks Tall's wife."

At that revelation, they just shook their heads, but no one was surprised. "That will do it," said Otter Tail.

"Is not his wife your sister, Howling Wolf?" asked She Bear Woman, who along with her sister and mother followed the quartet to the crowd.

Howling Wolf slowly nodded, then turned his attention back to Azariah. Gideon was growling at Stomps The Snake, but Azariah with a wave of his hand silenced him. Then he turned his attention back to the arrogant warrior, who was getting himself worked up for the fight.

"It doesn't have to end like this," signed Azariah. "Apologize for insulting my wife and I will forget the entire matter."

Stomps The Snake just laughed. "After I have your scalp hanging from my belt, white dog, and have your life, your Arapaho bitch is next!"

Azariah's blood was boiling again, but he kept his composure.

Howling Wolf approached him. "Make him suffer, brother," he said in Arapaho.

"For Sweet Grass, gladly!"

As the two combatants circled each other, Sparrow kept his hands on Gideon to keep him from interfering. Buffalo Hump announced that this was a fight to the death and a matter of honor. No one would interfere between Stomps The Snake and He Who Walks Tall. That was good enough for Azariah as he stood his ground and waited for Stomps The Snake to come to him. The Kainai warrior had already taken out his knife and had his war club in the other hand, but paused in confusion for a moment because Azariah had yet to take out his tomahawk and Arkansas toothpick.

No matter, Stomps The Snake thought to himself. He was not a man to waste such an opportunity, and without hesitation, charged at the bigger man.

Azariah had the advantage from the get-go. He quickly sidestepped Stomp The Snake, dodging a strike from the war club, and punched the warrior in the back of his head with a closed fist. The force from the punch dazed the warrior tremendously, knocking him completely off balance. But Stomps The Snake managed to quickly recover, turn, and go for a second charge, this time striking with his knife hand.

Azariah dodged that strike by jumping backward and then in a split second launched a wicked right hook to the Kainai warrior's jaw, this time knocking him to the ground, causing him to lose his grip on his weapons.

Again, Stomps The Snake was momentarily dazed. His head was spinning from the punch. When he regained his senses, he was shocked to see Azariah just standing there, still unarmed and grinning. It was clear to everyone what the giant trapper was doing. He was toying with the warrior, and this was not going to be a quick or merciful kill. If Stomps The Snake was looking for help or even sympathy from his own people, he was sadly mistaken. By this time, everyone knew the trapper known as He Who Walks Tall was defending the honor of his wife, who Stomps The Snake had insulted, and considering the fact that he and his friends were guests in this village, Stomps The Snake brought this mess on himself.

Azariah calmly kicked Stomps The Snake's war club to him and then backed off a little bit, as if waiting for his next move.

This only enraged the warrior as he angrily shouted, "I will not die at the hands of a white dog!" With that, he grabbed the war club and charged.

Azariah was through playing. He grabbed Stomps The Snake by the throat with one hand as he charged and grabbed the arm holding the war club with his other hand. In a split second, with all his might, Azariah bent that arm backwards, snapping it in two. Stomps The Snake howled in pain, but only for a second as the giant trapper quickly crushed his larynx with one squeeze. Despite hitting Azariah with his free hand, Stomps The Snake was doomed. Azariah never let up as he continued to tighten his grip around the warrior's throat until his neck snapped like a twig. Azariah finally let go, and Stomps The Snake's body fell to the ground. The fight was over.

Azariah stood victorious, but he was not celebrating. He looked around the Kainai crowd and in sign, said, "I did not want this. I gave him every opportunity to apologize for insulting my wife. I did not want to take his life, nor will I take his scalp."

The village was silent. Even some of Stomps The Snake's closest friends said nothing. Suddenly, an elderly couple came out of the crowd and approached Azariah. Although he dwarfed both of them, he was nervous.

"My son was the one who challenged you to a fight to the death," said the elderly man. "He was foolish in doing so and he was too proud, but he was still my son. He wasn't always like that."

Azariah signed, "I am sorry it ended like this."

The elder who was Stomps The Snake's father just nodded and then he, along with his wife, took their son's body back to their lodge to prepare him for burial. There were some angry faces, but no one could deny that Azariah was given little choice. Chief Buffalo Hump announced that there would be no retaliation taken against He Who Walks Tall or his friends. This was supported by the council and at that the crowd dispersed.

Gideon ran to his master, wagging his tail, followed by Howling Wolf, Beaver, Otter Tail and Sparrow who patted Azariah on the back for his victory.

"Do not feel sorry for what happened, brother," said Howling Wolf. "He left you little choice."

"I know," said Azariah. "I still wish it didn't have to end that way."

"Like his father said..." said Beaver, "he was foolish and too proud; he brought it on himself."

The quintet was suddenly approached by Chief Buffalo Hump, Kills The Enemy and Red Shield. "Come with us," signed the medicine man. "All of you."

17

At the Rendezvous at the Cheyenne village of Black Cloud, Liam O'Reilly was invited to dinner by Yellow Hawk. As he sat in the elder's lodge, Chokecherry Woman and her brother's wife, Sitting Fox Woman, had truly outdone themselves with their cooking. Everyone feasted on buffalo stew, which was Yellow Hawk's favorite, with some raspberry pudding for dessert. When everyone's belly was full, Yellow Hawk had his daughter bring his peace pipe. He lit the pipe and according to tradition, honored the four directions of Mother Earth before smoking it. He passed it to his son, Red Moon, who repeated the process before giving it to Liam, who also repeated the process and returned it to Yellow Hawk after he was done smoking it.

After the pipe was put away, the Cheyenne elder spoke. "How are our friends, the Arapaho?" he asked.

"Better than expected," answered Liam. "The family of He Who Walks Tall are still a little concerned, but they are confident that he will return."

"Not many men would do what He Who Walks Tall did," said Red Moon. "Especially for an enemy such as the Blackfeet."

"He Who Walks Tall has always been unique," said Liam. "Thinking of others more than himself, regardless whether they are friend or foe, is how he is and how he was raised."

"He Dog told me that He Who Walks Tall is the son of a white medicine man," added Yellow Hawk. "Is this true?"

"It is true," answered Liam. "But among the white men, holy men are not medicine men, but sort of like teachers that spread the message of the Creator. Medicine men are the healers of the sick and afflicted."

"Interesting," said Yellow Hawk.

The Cheyenne elder and his son always thought white men were very strange and peculiar people. At that moment, Bluebird and Little Fawn walked up to the men and sat next to Liam.

"Raging Bull," asked Little Fawn, "how come there are no white women with you white men?"

Liam laughed, while Yellow Hawk and Red Moon chuckled. Chokecherry Woman was a little embarrassed by her daughter's question but said nothing as she waited for Liam to answer the question. "That is a good question," he said. "I guess the reason white women do not come out West with us ugly white men is because they are not as strong as us to handle living out here in the wilderness."

"I have often wondered myself about the women of your kind, Raging Bull," said Red Moon "I have always wanted to meet one."

"Oh, you have, have you?" shouted Sitting Fox Woman.

"Uh-oh," said Liam.

Yellow Hawk grinned wickedly at his son. "Well, haven't you wondered or wanted to meet the women of Raging Bull's people?" asked Red Moon to his wife.

"Whether I wanted to or not is not the point," she responded. "My question is why are you so interested in meeting a white woman?"

Red Moon was dumbfounded and did not know how to answer his wife. When he turned to Liam and his father, they both raised up their arms and gave a "don't look at me" face.

"I am just curious, that is all," he said.

"Oh, I am not curious enough for you?" shouted Sitting Fox Woman.

"Woman, calm yourself," said Red Moon. "You are making a big fuss over nothing."

"Am I now?" said Sitting Fox Woman. "You have never admitted to being curious about white women before. Why now?"

"Maybe it is because I have never seen one!" shouted Red Moon. "You ever thought about that?"

Chokecherry Woman suddenly gave a loud whistle to get everyone's attention. "Sitting Fox Woman, I think you know my brother better than to think that he would ever bring another woman to his buffalo robes."

"Is that what you thought, wife?" said a surprised Red Moon.

Chokecherry Woman just shook her head in disbelief at her brother. "And you, Red Moon, really need to think before you speak, especially in front of your wife."

"What is that supposed to mean?"

"It means stop while you're ahead," laughed Liam.

"My son has a lot to learn about women," chuckled Yellow Hawk.

Red Moon, still with a dumbfounded look on his face, was trying to figure out what his father meant by that, when an angry Sitting Fox Woman stormed out of the lodge. "Excuse me," he said as he chased after her.

"How often does that happen?" asked Liam.

"Too often," answered Yellow Hawk. "Our young men these days, they have no clue when it comes to women."

"Raging Bull?" said Little Fawn.

"Yes?"

"You're not ugly."

The Irishman smiled and even blushed a little. "Why, thank you, Little Fawn. That is very nice of you to say."

Yellow Hawk beamed with pride at his youngest granddaughter, then slightly turned to her mother and found a small smile on her face.

Bluebird tugged on Liam's sleeve to get his attention. When he turned to her, she whispered in his ear and said, "I think Mother likes you very much."

The Irishman smiled and nodded as the two girls giggled. Chokecherry Woman suspected what her eldest daughter said to Liam. Between conversations, she and Liam exchanged glances, which didn't go unnoticed by Yellow Hawk, who looked on approvingly. At that moment, Red Moon and Sitting Fox Woman returned in much better spirits, much to the relief of everyone.

———

Back at the village of Buffalo Hump, Azariah, Beaver, Otter Tail, Howling Wolf, and Sparrow were sitting outside a lodge with Red Shield, Buffalo Hump, and Kills The Enemy. After the fight with Stomps The Snake, Red Shield had invited the quintet to do a sweat. This was a huge honor because they were considered enemies of the people. Never had a Blackfoot—warrior, holy man, chief, or elder—invited an enemy to do a sweat. It was clear to everyone that Red Shield held Azariah and his friends in high regard, and after the deadly fight with Stomps The Snake, which Azariah clearly tried to avoid, everyone guessed this was the reason behind Red Shield's invitation.

As the medicine man and his associates were preparing the sweat lodge, Buffalo Hump, Kills The Enemy, along with Azariah and his friends struck up a conversation.

"Tell me, He Who Walks Tall," signed Kills The Enemy. "Your woman obviously means a lot to you."

Azariah nodded. "She means the world to me, for she is my heart."

"That is why you accepted Stomps The Snake's challenge when he insulted her," signed Kills The Enemy. Azariah knew it was a statement, not a question. "I can't say I would have done any different."

"Have you ever done a sweat before, He Who Walks Tall?" asked Buffalo Hump through sign. Azariah shook his head. "What about the rest of you?"

Everyone except Otter Tail and Sparrow shook their head.

"I have done a sweat on many occasions," signed Otter Tail.

"I did my first one last summer," signed Sparrow.

"It is good to do a sweat," said Buffalo Hump. "Especially when the soul is troubled, it needs to be cleansed."

"You five should be honored," added Kills The Enemy. "We have never done this for an enemy."

"It is strange, don't you think?" signed Azariah. "After all that has happened, we will still be enemies."

"It is, He Who Walks Tall," said Buffalo Hump. "But that is the way of things."

"I wish it didn't have to be that way," said Azariah. "People can change if they try."

"For a white man, He Who Walks Tall, you are truly interesting," said Kills The Enemy. "You would rather live in peace with your enemies than in conflict."

"If it means keeping those that I love and care about safe, then so be it."

"Thinking that way is not wrong," said Buffalo Hump. "But any man who wishes to live in peace with his enemies would have a better chance of capturing the wind."

"Sad but true," signed Howling Wolf. "But I share my white brother's feelings, and I pray that after today, we can at least be friends with the people of Buffalo Hump and Kills The Enemy."

At that, both brothers smiled and nodded their approval.

"We are ready now," said Red Shield.

18

The next morning, Azariah was up at the crack of dawn and had quietly exited the lodge of Buffalo Hump to think. The sweat lodge had changed him. He felt as if a small weight was lifted off his shoulders. During the sweat, Red Shield counseled him to let go—let go of his pain, his past that continued to haunt him, and to not mistake vengeance for justice, because it would consume him and all those who love him by turning him into the monster he hates.

Azariah was thinking about that when Buffalo Hump appeared behind him. The giant trapper nearly jumped out of his moccasins. The Kainai chief laughed. "There are a few people in this world that can sneak up on me like that," said Azariah. "My children among them."

"How many children do you have?" asked Buffalo Hump.

"Two," answered Azariah. "A boy who has seen six summers and a girl who is now in her second winter."

"Children are a blessing from the Napi," said Buffalo Hump. "It is said that when they are born, they are a spitting image of their father."

"I have never heard of that," said Azariah.

"It is true," responded Buffalo Hump. "It is nature's way of saying that you are the father." The chief paused for a moment as he welcomed the sun rising. "Tell me, He Who Walks Tall, do your children look like you?"

Azariah nodded. "I wished they looked more like their mother instead of my ugly face."

At that Buffalo Hump just laughed. "Walk with me."

As they walked through the village, everyone was getting up and active. Some had gone to the nearby lake to wash up, others were welcoming the rising sun. Buffalo Hump was in deep thought before he and Azariah came upon the two prisoners, Charles Bundy and Dick Dahmer, both still staked to the ground, spread-eagled.

"Our women shall deliver justice on these two dogs for what they have done," signed Buffalo Hump.

"I long to see them suffer," responded Azariah.

The chief slowly shook his head. "You and your brothers have done enough," he said. "You shall leave today and return to your families among the Cheyenne and Arapaho."

Before Azariah could ask why he wouldn't be allowed to see justice done, Buffalo Hump took him by the arm away from the condemned prisoners. "Tell me about your woman," he said.

"Her name is Sweet Grass," said Azariah. "Her father is a sub-chief and elder among their people."

"She must be some woman," said Buffalo Hump, "that you would kill to protect her honor."

"I would kill to protect her and our children," responded Azariah. "As any man would."

"Not every man, He Who Walks Tall," said Buffalo Hump.

They walked to the edge of the village. By this time the sun was fully up and the two stood in silence for a moment. "I have seen many of our women lose their hearts and heads to trappers," said Buffalo Hump. "And I have seen some trappers lose their hearts and heads to our women, and I have yet to see any of those situations end well."

"I have seen the same at Rendezvous and even among my adopted tribe," said Azariah. He knew where the Kainai chief was going with this. He knew that white men like himself and Liam O'Reilly were the exception to the rule. He knew trappers who had taken Indian women for a season or two, then abandoned them and their mixed-blood children as they returned to civilization. Some of these men had wives and children back in the settlements that the Indian women didn't even know about. Azariah frowned upon such men and usually kept them at arm's length. Despite his youth, he took marriage and fatherhood very seriously and had no regrets marrying Sweet Grass and fathering their children. His family was his pride and joy, and he couldn't imagine leaving them nor could he understand why any real man would abandon his wife and kids. In his mind, it was not right and unforgivable.

"You mentioned a twin sister," signed Buffalo Hump. "Do have other family?"

"A mother and a father," answered Azariah. "Back in the land of the whites."

"They still live?"

Azariah just shrugged. "I wish I knew because I would love to see them again."

Buffalo Hump raised an eyebrow. He understood that Azariah was very close to his family. "Would they approve of your woman and your children?"

Azariah had to think for a minute. "To honest with you, I do not know," he said. "My parents taught me to treat people as people. Skin color is not important."

Buffalo Hump had a slightly surprised look on his face. "Every white man I have met believes the opposite."

"That is because most white parents don't teach their children the same way my parents taught me," admitted Azariah. "My family are the exception. That is why we were so hated among our people."

This intrigued Buffalo Hump. "Hated?"

"Among my people, my father is a holy man, but not a very popular one," explained Azariah. "He speaks against the practice of slavery and that according to the Creator, we are all related, regardless of skin color or even who we worship."

The Kainai chief rubbed his chin in thought. Never had he heard of a white man teach such radical belief that all men are related and equal in the eyes of the Napi. He never even heard of a white medicine man, at that; now he was talking to the son of one. The more he learned about Azariah, the more he began to actually like the man. "It is a shame that you are not a Blackfoot, He Who Walks Tall."

The giant trapper smiled. "Born a Blackfoot or adopted?" The chief laughed. "I wanted to ask you," said Azariah. "How come you want us to leave before those two dogs are executed?"

"Because you and your brothers have done enough," answered Buffalo Hump. "You saved my daughters and my niece and returned them to us along with those men who caused them pain." Buffalo Hump returned his gaze back to the sun and then lowered his head for a moment. "Return to your families," he said. "They need you more than ever and are probably worried about you."

Azariah was silent for a moment. He found great respect for the Kainai chief and deep in his heart, he was saddened that they were still enemies and not friends. He wished that could change, not just between them, but between their people as well. Both knew that was impossible. "I thank you for your kindness and wisdom, Buffalo Hump," signed Azariah.

The chief nodded as he and the trapper walked back to his lodge. When they returned, Howling Wolf, Beaver, Otter Tail, and Sparrow were up and about with the chief's family. Sparrow was chatting with White Flower through sign. They were laughing and chuckling much to Little Bird's annoyance. Buffalo Hump had a look of interest on his face as he stared down the young Cheyenne warrior, who appeared to be wooing his youngest daughter. White Flower bowed her head, but continued smiling, while Sparrow, who looked like a kid that got caught with his hand in the cookie jar, gave a nervous acknowledgment of the chief's presence.

Azariah, Howling Wolf, Beaver, and Otter Tail were chuckling themselves up a storm at their friend's awkward predicament. "It is good that we are leaving today, my brothers," said Azariah. Everyone had a look of relief on their faces —everyone except Sparrow.

"So soon?" he asked.

"Buffalo Hump and his people have been gracious hosts to us, considering the circumstances," said Azariah in Cheyenne. "Let's not give them a reason to think they were wrong in doing so."

Sparrow sheepishly bowed his head as he understood what Azariah meant by his statement. "When do we leave?"

19

Back at the Cheyenne village of Black Cloud near the Rendezvous, Liam O'Reilly and Chokecherry Woman were walking near the lake. Since dinner the night before, they had gotten closer than ever.

"Tell me about where you're from," asked Chokecherry Woman.

Since there was no word for 'Ireland' or 'Boston' in the Cheyenne tongue, Liam had to improvise, but it wasn't much of a challenge for him since he spoke Cheyenne fluently. "There is not much to tell," he said. "Other than where I was born and where I grew up are as different as night and day."

"Truly?" asked Chokecherry Woman.

The Irishman nodded. "Ireland," he said in English before switching back to Cheyenne, "is as beautiful as the land of the Cheyenne and many other tribes; there are mountains almost as tall as the Shining Mountains and just as beautiful." Even though he left Ireland when he was ten years old, he remembered the country of his birth clearly. "Boston is the exact opposite."

"How so?" asked Chokecherry Woman.

Liam had to think for a moment. His childhood memories of Boston weren't all bad, but they weren't heavenly either. "The best way I can describe it is smothered."

Chokecherry Woman had a surprised look on her face at the description of the childhood home of Raging Bull.

"White people don't move around a lot to find hunting grounds or raid enemies," said Liam. "Everything they want or need is in one place, unlike out here."

"How do you protect yourselves from enemies?" asked Chokecherry Woman.

"The threats to our way of life or to our loved ones are more from within the city than from outside," answered Liam. "This is one of the reasons I left and came out here to be a trapper."

"Don't you miss your family, though?" asked Chokecherry Woman.

Liam smiled as he looked around and back at the village. "The Cheyenne are my family and my people now, as well as He Who Walks Tall and his family."

Chokecherry Woman smiled at that statement and gently touched the Irishman's long red hair, which was starting to grow some strands of gray but not a lot. Liam closed his eyes as he felt his blood grow hot from her touch. When he opened them, he turned to her and looked deeply into her dark brown eyes.

"You not like my touch?" she asked.

"I like your touch very much, Chokecherry Woman," he answered. "I care for you and your daughters very much, but last time I gave my heart to someone, she and our baby were taken from me. I am so afraid of that happening again."

Chokecherry Woman bowed her head for a moment before returning her gaze back to Liam. "I know the pain of losing someone you loved dearly," she said. "But we cannot live our life in fear; if so, then we will never learn to live, and that is a life worse than death." She took his hand and placed it over her chest and gave him a smile. "My heart is yours, Raging Bull," she said. "I will not let anything or anyone take you from me."

At that, Liam took Chokecherry Woman's hand and placed it on his chest. "And mine belongs to you and you alone," he said. "For as long I live and there is a Creator watching over us, I will never leave you, and I will love your daughters as if they were my own."

Suddenly he kissed her on the lips. Before he had the chance to release the kiss, she wrapped her arms around him to prolong it. So much were they into their passion, they didn't realize they had an audience in the form of Bluebird and Little Fawn who were giggling at their mother and their soon-to-be stepfather. The couple released their embrace upon hearing the girls' laughter, to which Liam responded with a smile.

"I have a question for you, Bluebird and Little Fawn," he said. "How would you like to have me as your new father?"

The girls responded by running to Liam and giving him a hug. He responded by wrapping his arms around them and scooping them up in a bear hug before putting them back down. He then let go with one arm and put it around Chokecherry Woman and pulled her close as he made it official. They were going to be a family.

————

At the Arapaho village of White Antelope, Sweet Grass came back from visiting the families of Beaver and Otter Tail. Everyone was worried about Azariah and the boys. Even though it was a long trek to the land of the Blackfeet, the fear of whether they had been killed was on everyone's mind. The fact that Azariah had taken three Blackfoot girls back to their people didn't surprise anyone. It was one of the reasons he was called He Who Walks Tall, and he lived up to that name in more ways than one and more times than anyone could count. Nor did it surprise anyone that Beaver and Otter Tail volunteered to accompany him to the land of the Blackfeet to return those girls, for everyone knew that the trio was the closest of friends and they would watch out for each other no matter what.

Otter Tail's wife and parents mentioned as much to Sweet Grass in order to give comfort and encouragement. Wandering Bear, the medicine man, and his daughter, Bird Feather, also encouraged Sweet Grass and the rest of the families to have faith and hope.

"The Man Above has not brought your husband, brother, and Beaver and Otter Tail this far only to have them taken from us now," said Wandering Bear. "They will return to us."

"You sound like my son," said Sweet Grass. "I wish I had your confidence."

The elder just smiled. He had known Sweet Grass her entire life, for he was not only good friends with her father but was also a surrogate uncle to her. He was also one of a handful of people who encouraged the marriage union between her and Azariah because he believed that the two were truly meant to be together as chosen by the Man Above. Wandering Bear was grateful that his intuition had been correct. He had seen how happy both Sweet Grass and He Who Walks Tall had been over the years and the kind of parents they were to their two young children. The Arapaho medicine man had also become a sort of spiritual advisor to Azariah and Sweet Grass, especially during the dark times, when the former was haunted by bad dreams and demons from his past. When Azariah needed someone to talk to, if he couldn't talk to his wife, Wandering Bear was the next best thing. His counsel was greatly appreciated, and it helped a lot.

But deep down, even the medicine man worried like the rest of the people. He prayed to the Man Above that He Who Walks Tall's compassion didn't get him and those who followed him killed. Like many warriors, he had heard of the Kainai chief, Buffalo Hump, and his hot-headed brother, Kills The Enemy. If they were true men of honor, they would repay He Who Walks Tall, Howling Wolf, Beaver, Otter Tail, and Sparrow for rescuing their women and returning them, by sparing their lives and allowing them to return to their loved ones among the people.

Sweet Grass had given a lot of thought to what Wandering Bear had said and she too prayed that he was right. She couldn't imagine living without Azariah. There was no room in her heart for another man, for he was one of kind. She thought about her children. How would they live without their father? At that same moment, she quickly removed the thought. "Get control of yourself," she said to herself. "Your husband and brother will return. They are warriors and the Man Above will bring them home."

"Who are you talking to, Ma?" asked Adam. The young boy had startled his mother as she was trying to get a grip. She looked at her firstborn and only son with great pride. She couldn't believe that he was now six winters old but had the maturity of boys much older than him. She noticed that he had great faith that his father would return, and she wished she had half as much he did.

"I was just talking to myself and thinking, Bear Claw," she said as she called him by his Arapaho name.

"About Pa?"

Sweet Grass nodded as she gently placed her hand on his head. "Where is your sister?"

"With Grandfather and Grandmother," answered Adam. "They were worried about Pa, too."

"He will return to us, Bear Claw," said Sweet Grass.

"I know," said Adam with look of confidence. "God is with him."

Sweet Grass was surprised but said nothing. She and Azariah had often talked about the religion with each other and while she herself never claimed her husband's Christianity, she respected it and was not against him teaching it to their children. In fact, it was never an issue, because Azariah greatly respected the religious beliefs of the Arapaho and Cheyenne and believed that Christians and most Indian tribes worshipped the same God, they just called Him by name in different languages. This was something most whites, especially those claiming to be Christians, rejected, mostly out of racial ignorance than religious beliefs. Sweet Grass knew this, mainly because Azariah and Liam told her this not long after they both taught her how to read and write. The Bible was one of the very first books Azariah taught Sweet Grass how to read, and he did his best in answering all questions she had about Jesus Christ and those who followed him. She knew that a lot of the teachings and beliefs that her husband had he learned from his parents. It was that reason alone why she did not object to Azariah teaching and sharing the faith of his people to their children. As far as she was concerned, her husband's parents were his people and from what she was told about them, they were at least the only ones who followed the teachings of the One called Jesus Christ.

While Azariah did not force his religious beliefs on Sweet Grass and the children, he did talk about them and did his best to live by them. On many occasions, he even had friendly discussions about it with Wandering Bear, which were usually initiated when the medicine man had questions. Other than that, he was someone who would rather live by the word than teach it. Sweet Grass remembered the stories her husband told her concerning his parents and what they were like. Plus, when she started reading the Bible, despite the questions she had and probably didn't fully believe in it, she did find it helpful when it came to everyday life. She even had favorite stories—one being the story of Ruth. It reminded her of herself and Azariah. She remembered how he blushed when she told him. That is what she missed the most, even though he hadn't been gone that long. The quiet moments they had. If Jesus Christ and the Man Above are truly one in the same, then she prayed without ceasing to Him that He would bring her man home and all those who went with him safe and sound.

20

That same day at the Kainai village of Buffalo Hump, Azariah, Howling Wolf, Beaver, Otter Tail, and Sparrow were preparing to leave to return home. While Azariah wanted to see Bundy and Dahmer tortured to death by the Blackfeet women for what they had done, he took to heart what Red Shield and Buffalo Hump said to him, plus he and his friends did not want to overstay their welcome, especially since Sparrow had been talking to Buffalo Hump's youngest daughter, White Flower. Also, they truly missed their families and felt that it was time to return to them, while they still could. Despite that the council had voted to spare their lives and allow them to return to their people, there were still a few hotheads who wanted their scalps, especially Azariah's since he was considered big medicine.

Some of the hotheads, like Blue Duck, were friends of

Stomp The Snake, but unlike him, he was no fool. Blue Duck was a capable and brave Kainai warrior in his own right, but he knew his limitations. Stomp The Snake tried to defy his own limitations, which got him killed for his efforts. Blue Duck was a man who picked and chose his battles wisely. He wouldn't openly defy the council, but he knew once the giant trapper and his Arapaho brethren left the safety of the village, they would eventually be fair game.

He was discussing his thoughts with some of his friends when they were approached by Dog Star.

"What are all of you planning?" asked Dog Star.

Blue Duck just smirked at the young warrior. He was older than him by a few years and while they were not hostile to each other, they were not exactly friends. "Nothing that concerns you," said Blue Duck. "We are just talking about possibly going on a hunt this afternoon."

Blue Duck's friends chuckled, but Dog Star would not be put off. He knew that Blue Duck and Stomps The Snake were close; that the latter wanted revenge for his friend's death.

"As long as the hunt doesn't have anything to do with He Who Walks Tall," said Dog Star.

"I would never think that you would be a friend to a white man," scoffed Blue Duck.

"Maybe I am, maybe I am not," responded Dog Star. "I do know that the council has spoken and voted that He Who Walks Tall and his friends were not to be harmed in any way, shape or form, and it would be foolish to defy the council—Buffalo Hump and Kills The Enemy in particular."

Blue Duck turned and stared down the young warrior. "You calling me a fool?!"

"He didn't say that," said Kills The Enemy as he came from behind a lodge. He had been listening to the entire conversation and came between Dog Star and Blue Duck. "He said it would be foolish for anyone to defy the council," he said. "It would be foolish to defy my brother and me as well."

Blue Duck's cousin, Yellow Weasel, immediately but gently grabbed his arm to get him to back down. The hothead yanked away his arm but had the common sense not to challenge Kills The Enemy. "So we let our enemies leave just like that?"

"Just like that, and best leave it like that," said Kills The Enemy.

Azariah and his friends were all packed and ready. The village gathered to see them off. They thanked Chief Buffalo Hump and his family for their hospitality and also showed gratitude to Red Shield and the council for their wisdom and kindness. She Bear Woman, White Flower, and Star Watcher had hugged each of them and expressed their gratitude for returning them to their people and also bringing the men who kidnapped them to face justice. Kills The Enemy and Dog Star had just arrived through the crowd to see them off as well.

"Be careful as you head home, He Who Walks Tall," said Dog Star. "There are those among us who are not happy with the council's decision to let you and your friends live."

"He speaks the truth," added Kills The Enemy.

Buffalo Hump raised his eyebrow at what his brother and the young warrior said and turned his attention towards a group of warriors standing far from the crowd. He noticed Blue Duck at the head of them, looking unhappy.

The chief returned his attention back to the trapper and his friends. "Keep eyes on your backtrail," he said.

Azariah and Howling Wolf noticed Blue Duck and his friends also and took seriously what Buffalo Hump, Kills The Enemy, and Dog Star had said. "Thank you," signed Azariah. "All of you will forever have our deepest gratitude."

"We will keep an eye out for any danger," added Howling Wolf. Beaver and Otter Tail were already on their mounts, eager to get going. Gideon was also eager, wagging his tail as he waited for his master. Sparrow had a solemn look on his face as he said his farewell to White Flower. She too was solemn, but they both knew that a future between them was not going to happen. He was Cheyenne and she was Blackfoot. Their people were bitter enemies. It wouldn't work out.

"Time to go, Sparrow," said Azariah in Cheyenne. He then turned back to Buffalo Hump and Kills The Enemy. "Next time we meet," he signed, "I hope it will be as friends, not enemies."

"Unlikely," signed Buffalo Hump. "But a man can hope."

"I am happy to say that as far as white men go," added Kills The Enemy, "I am proud to call you one who is truly honorable."

Azariah accepted that and offered his hand to Kills The Enemy, who accepted it. He repeated the process with Buffalo Hump, Dog Star and Red Shield. He, Howling Wolf, and Sparrow mounted up. Azariah signaled Gideon, pointing south, and the dog trotted ahead of the quintet as they headed out of the Kainai village. Azariah paused for a moment and then turned and waved back at the villagers, who whooped and cheered in return.

After Azariah and his brethren left, the village of Buffalo Hump turned their attention to Charles Bundy and Richard Dahmer, still staked out to the ground. The women, all armed with knives, proceeded to deliver justice to the villains who caused pain to She Bear Woman, White Flower, and Star Watcher. Dahmer, already ill from the infection from the bullet wound in his backside, was already numbed and had surrendered to his doom. Bundy, despite his pain from his missing ear, tried to show a brave front and even spat at the women who were about to skin him and Dahmer alive. In reality, he was terrified and did not want to meet his Maker. When the first woman grabbed his manhood to cut it off, the last thing that was on his mind was, "Why me?"

21

As they traveled through the plains from the Kainai village, Azariah and his friends were excited to finally be on their way home, but they did not let down their guard, not until they were satisfied that they were out of Blackfoot country completely. Taking Buffalo Hump's advice, Azariah continued to watch their backtrail, while Gideon was ahead in the lead, followed by Otter Tail. Everyone was slightly nervous. Despite trusting in the word of the Kainai council, they knew that Blue Duck and some of his friends would probably be wanting revenge for the death of Stomps The Snake and would be coming after them.

After the torture and execution of Charles Bundy and Richard Dahmer, Blue Duck was secretly plotting with Yellow Weasel and a couple of others who wanted to make a name for themselves. Most, like Yellow Weasel, had nothing personal against He Who Walks Tall or his friends, other than that they were enemies of the people and that the former was well known and popular among nearly all the tribes of the Northern Plains. Any warrior, Blackfoot or otherwise, who managed to kill the giant trapper with red hair would be the envy of his people. That is what some of the warriors who disagreed with the council's decision were after—glory and big medicine.

The next morning before the sun rose, Blue Duck, Yellow Weasel, and six other warriors left the village carefully and quietly so that they didn't wake up anyone or arouse suspicion and headed south. They knew that He Who Walks Tall was headed towards Bear Lake, where the gathering of trappers was taking place, and they wanted to catch him and his friends before they arrived.

Azariah was just waking up to answer nature's call. He had his belt pistol and Arkansas toothpick with him just in case as he went to relieve himself. It was not smart to let your guard down in the wilderness, for while they were still in Blackfoot country, the tribe was not the only thing that grated on the young trapper's nerves that morning. Wild critters were up and about as well, from a pack of wolves to the mighty grizzly bear. The last one is what Azariah was most concerned about. He had a healthy fear of the big bruins, going all the way back almost eight years previously, when he had his first encounter with a grizzly. He was still a greenhorn and only fourteen years old when he killed the beast with his blunderbuss before it collapsed on top of him. Liam O'Reilly was there when it happened and said it was the biggest grizzly he had ever seen, which is why Azariah considered it either dumb luck or divine providence that he survived the experience. After relieving himself, he gently touched the bear claws around his neck belonging to that great beast that almost devoured him. Since then he had had at least five encounters with grizzlies, three of them she-bears with cubs, and he did not care to have another run-in with them ever again for as long as he lived.

Lost in his thoughts, he didn't notice Howling Wolf come up from behind him, and he almost pulled out his pistol as his brother-in-law startled him.

"I must be losing it."

"Losing what?" asked Howling Wolf.

"My senses," answered Azariah. "That is the second time this trip someone has been able to sneak up on me like that."

"Maybe it is your whiteness," laughed Howling Wolf.

"Very funny," sneered Azariah.

Howling Wolf chuckled then got a little serious. "Something is bothering you this morning."

Azariah turned towards the darkness and shrugged. "Just a feeling."

"That we're being followed," said Howling Wolf.

Azariah knew it was a statement, not a question. "We are still in Blackfoot country," he said. "But they are not my only worry."

Howling Wolf noticed that Azariah was touching his bear claw necklace. "I would not be surprised if there is a grizzly bear or two out their looking for breakfast," said Howling Wolf.

"That is not very comforting," said Azariah.

Howling Wolf gave his brother-in-law a serious look that turned into a slight smile. "It wasn't meant to be, my brother."

Unlike Azariah, Howling Wolf, along with Beaver, Otter Tail, and Sparrow, was born and raised in the wilderness. While he too had a healthy fear of the great grizzly bears that his people shared the wilderness with, he also had a sense of respect for them and for how the Man Above created them. While the Arapaho warrior was only older than his brother-in-law by two years, he was more mature and also understood that animals such as the grizzlies and the equally dangerous mountain lions did what was natural to them. He gave them a wide berth, but he did not let his fear of such dangerous animals control him.

"How do you do it?" asked Azariah.

"Do what?"

"Control your fear," asked Azariah. "There are times that I fear not just for myself, but for Sweet Grass and our children, wondering if some grizzly or mountain lion or a wolverine is going to pay us a visit."

"I asked my father that same question," said Howling Wolf, "when a grizzly bear almost took his life."

"What did he say?"

"That it is natural to be afraid," said Howling Wolf. "It is what makes us human, but so is learning to control your fear, not just of dangerous animals, but enemies of the two-legged variety as well."

Azariah smirked a little as they returned to the campfire. Beaver and Otter Tail were just waking up. Sparrow was still in la-la land, probably dreaming of White Flower, thought Howling Wolf. Azariah started the fire back up by adding twigs and leaves to it, while Beaver volunteered to take the coffee pot and head to the nearby lake to collect water to make more coffee.

Azariah advised his friend to be careful and return quickly, for they might pack up and head on out.

"But the sun is just rising," said Otter Tail.

"We're still in Blackfoot country, and I want to put as much distance between us and any possible war party on the prowl," said Azariah. "Plus I am really anxious to get back to Rendezvous to our families."

"Makes sense," agreed Otter Tail.

Howling Wolf woke up Sparrow, who wasn't too pleased at being disturbed. "I was having a good dream," he said using sign language before yawning.

"About Buffalo Hump's daughter, no doubt," said Azariah in Cheyenne. Everyone laughed while the young warrior gave a sheepish grin.

Gideon who had been out on one of his morning hunts, returned with a dead rabbit in his mouth. A couple of minutes later, Beaver also returned with a full pot of water and put it over the fire to heat it up, while Azariah added coffee beans to it. At that moment, while the sun was rising, the feeling that Azariah had earlier returned, and it began to bother him. This did not go unnoticed by anyone; even the dog sensed something was amiss.

"We best have our breakfast quick, then pack up and move," said Azariah. "You think the Blackfeet from Buffalo Hump's village are following us, He Who Walks Tall?" asked Otter Tail in Arapaho.

Azariah nodded. "I am praying that is all who is following us."

22

Later that noon, Blue Duck and his warriors found the abandoned camp of their quarry. Black Hand, who one of the best trackers, led them through a shorter path, before finding their tracks. "They haven't been gone long," he said in Blackfoot. "Probably left early this morning."

"They know we are following them," said Blue Duck. "He Who Walks Tall is truly no fool, for a white man."

"All the more reason we shouldn't have defied the council," said Yellow Weasel.

"I want his head, cousin," said Blue Duck angrily.

Yellow Weasel was no coward and he wanted big medicine, but he began to have second thoughts, and he was not afraid or ashamed to let his cousin know it. "I know Stomps The Snake was your best friend, but he got himself killed by challenging He Who Walks Tall," he said. "Not to mention that He Who Walks Tall gave him every chance to back down, for he did not wish to take his life."

"I was there, remember?" said Blue Duck. "It makes no difference. He is still an enemy to the people, no matter how honorable or how big his medicine is."

"And just how do you plan on explaining to Buffalo Hump and Kills The Enemy?" asked Soaring Bird. "They, along with the council, were specifically clear that He Who Walks Tall and his brethren were not to be harmed."

Blue Duck just scoffed. "Once we have their scalps along with their heads parading around the village, the people will see reason and show that our medicine is strong, even stronger than Buffalo Hump and Kills The Enemy."

Yellow Weasel and Soaring Bird did not like the sound of that and thought Blue Duck was letting his pride get the best of him. They had no love for He Who Walks Tall or his Arapaho and Cheyenne brethren, but they had respect for their chief and elders.

"We best go," said Black Hand. "The tracks lead south towards Bear Lake. If we don't catch them before they get there, then it will be too late."

"Agreed," said Blue Duck. "Are you warriors still with me?"

Everyone except Yellow Weasel and Soaring Bird whooped, but not wanting to have their courage or manhood questioned, they reluctantly nodded and said, "We are with you."

As Azariah and his men continued south through a pass into the mountains, Azariah's sixth sense started to kick in again and he wasn't alone. Gideon suddenly stopped and growled down their backtrail.

"Just as I thought," said Azariah. "We're being followed."

"The question is," said Howling Wolf, "by who or by what?"

The quintet continued down the pass until they found a suitable spot to make their stand. They were not far from the Beartooth Mountains where the trapper made his home and which was also Crow country, but that didn't make things any easier. The Crows were enemies of the Arapaho and Cheyenne as much as the Blackfeet were. Also they were notoriously known to be expert horse thieves, and neither Azariah or his friends were in the mood to be left stranded by having their horses stolen from them.

Blue Duck and his warriors were catching up on their quarry. The tracks had led to a pass going towards the Beartooth Mountains into Crow country, their most hated enemies. However, that didn't stop or slow them down. Black Hand was in the lead and following the tracks, when all of a sudden his horse got spooked and whinnied as it went on its hind legs, throwing him off. When he got up, he immediately saw the cause as an angry, full grown she-grizzly was charging towards him at full speed. He didn't have time to turn and run, and by the time he had out his knife, the she-beast was on him. His face was in her mouth, and in a split second, it was no more.

Blue Duck and the other warriors heard the screams and managed to ride up to their friend and tracker, but it was too late. Soaring Bird let loose an arrow at the grizzly, which found its mark, but instead of killing her, it only enraged her. She turned her attention to the new threat from the remaining seven Kainai warriors, who were trying to let loose more arrows into her, but their frantic horses were making it difficult.

Yellow Weasel was immediately bucked off his horse and landed head-first on a rock, which busted his skull wide open. Already in full fury from having ten arrows and counting shot into her and the smell of fresh blood increasing her blood lust, the she-grizzly went straight for Yellow Weasel, who was bleeding like a stuck pig.

Seeing his cousin badly hurt and about to be mauled, Blue Duck kicked his horse in a gallop and tried to get himself between the enraged bruin and his injured cousin. However, in so doing, the she-grizzly bulldozed her way into both horse and rider, knocking off the latter and causing him to fly at least ten feet before he crash-landed and was knocked unconscious. The horse got the worst of it, being sliced at the jugular from the grizzly's huge claws. Soaring Bird managed to grab control of his horse, got his lance, and launched the weapon straight into the grizzly's thick hide, piercing her lungs. Mortally wounded, the she-grizzly still had enough fight left in her and went straight for Soaring Bird. At that split moment, a gunshot rang and the she-grizzly collapsed at the feet of the Kainai warrior.

The remaining warriors got control of their horses and let loose a couple more arrows into the bear to make sure she was dead. Her three cubs, who were hiding in a thicket, were now up a tree, fearing that the warriors might come after them. Soaring Bird and the surviving members of the war party were searching for where that gunshot came from, after they were satisfied the grizzly was dead.

They looked to the south not far from them and saw riders headed towards them. It was He Who Walks Tall and his brethren. They pulled their horses to a stop in front of the Blackfeet. Sparrow had Black Hand's horse and moved forward to return it to them. They looked at the carnage and speculated what happened. Azariah gave the hand sign for peace and friendship. Soaring Bird responded in kind. He had the rest of the warriors check on Blue Duck and they returned with bad news. The vengeful warrior was impaled on a log that went through his sternum. He was dead within seconds.

"I hope you are just a hunting party," signed Azariah to Soaring Bird.

The warrior gave a sad look and shook his head. "We were hunting He Who Walks Tall," he signed. "But we were hunting you against the wishes of our chief and elders."

Gideon growled, while Howling Wolf, Beaver, Otter Tail, and Sparrow aimed their rifles in a ready-to-shoot position at the Blackfeet.

"Was it your rifle that killed the bear?" asked Soaring Bird.

"No," answered Azariah. "It was my brother's rifle, Howling Wolf."

Howling Wolf rode up to Soaring Bird, not taking his rifle from its position.

"How did you know?" asked Soaring Bird in sign.

"We had a feeling that we were being followed," Azariah signed back. "We were waiting for you in pass ahead, when one of your horses rode past frightened."

"And you came back in time to help us from the grizzly?" asked Soaring Bird.

"We didn't do it for you," said Howling Wolf in sign. "We did it for Buffalo Hump."

Soaring Bird and the remaining Kainai warriors nodded their understanding. "Know this, He Who Walks Tall," said Soaring Bird, "Blue Duck was the one who wanted to defy the council and take your scalp and those of your brethren, while some of us, myself included, wanted to gain glory and big medicine." Soaring Bird paused for a moment as he now looked at the dead bodies of Black Hand and Yellow Weasel, then hearing that Blue Duck was also dead, he and the rest of the war party had come to see the folly of their decision. "We were wrong," he signed. "Go in peace. We will not follow."

At that, Azariah signed his thanks, while Howling Wolf, Otter Tail, Beaver, and Sparrow lowered their rifles. Gideon stopped growling as Azariah signaled him to head south as he and his friends followed.

23

One week later at Bear Lake, the Rendezvous was still in full swing. Liam O'Reilly, accompanied by Chokecherry Woman and her daughters, visited Sweet Grass and her family to not only announce their engagement but to also plan together a rescue party to find Azariah and their friends. Everyone feared the worst, when suddenly Adam looked off into the north of the village and in distance saw them riding in.

"Pa!" he shouted and was about to run and greet his father, but Sweet Grass was already running at top speed, surpassing her son.

She ran as fast as her legs could carry her, while Azariah immediately slowed his horse to a stop, jumped off and greeted his beloved wife as she jumped into his arms. They kissed passionately for a long time as Howling Wolf, Beaver, Otter Tail, and Sparrow just sat on their horses, grinning from ear to ear at the happy reunion. Gideon ran towards the village to greet the kids and quickly tackled Adam, licking his face, while Clay Basket and Two Hawks were carrying Sara and Little Badger to greet the returning rescue party. Prairie Bird Woman also ran and was greeted by her husband as he jumped down from his horse and held her in his arms. By this time word had spread around the village that Azariah, Howling Wolf, Beaver, Otter Tail, and the Cheyenne warrior, Sparrow, had returned from the land of the Blackfeet and everyone had come out to greet them.

Azariah had let go of his wife long enough to scoop up both of his children into his arms and give them a huge hug and kissed both of them on their foreheads. Howling Wolf hugged his parents and was handed his son and thanked the Man Above as he held Little Badger high above his head. Beaver and Otter Tail were greeted by their families in traditional Arapaho fashion and then greeted by Chief White Antelope, his grandson, Lone Wolf, and the medicine man, Wandering Bear, and his family.

It was truly good to be finally home and Azariah looked up into the sky and gave a silent thanks to the Almighty for the safe return.

"I knew you would come back, Pa!" shouted Adam as he hugged his father's neck.

"And I will never leave you, your sister, or your mother ever again," said Azariah in Arapaho.

At hearing that, Sweet Grass wrapped her arms around

her man's waist as tears streamed down her cheeks. Azariah gently put down Adam and Sara to wipe away their mother's tears. Speaking to her in Arapaho, he said, "For as I live and as long as you will have me, I will never leave your side again."

"Then you are mine forever," responded Sweet Grass.

At that exact moment, Liam O'Reilly cleared his throat in mock anger. "Am I invisible now?" he said. "Your missus and wee ones are not the only family members that have been worried sick about you."

Everyone laughed as Azariah gave his best friend a bear hug, followed by Beaver, Otter Tail, and Sparrow, who greeted the Irishman with hugs as well.

"Uncle Liam is getting married, Pa," said Adam all of a sudden.

"He is what?"

"Now that the little runt has spoiled the surprise," said Liam in mock anger. "You remember Chokecherry Woman and her daughters?"

Azariah was truly surprised as the Irishman introduced his new bride-to-be and future step-daughters. Sparrow whooped in celebration at the revelation, for he knew that his father and grandfather were trying to get Liam to remarry for quite some time, since Liam's late wife was his aunt.

"Well, it is about time," said Azariah. "Congratulations and welcome to the family, Chokecherry Woman." Forgetting that she didn't speak English, Azariah repeated his words in Cheyenne and Chokecherry Woman thanked him.

Sweet Grass also welcomed the new bride-to-be and her two daughters with a hug and then signed, "It will truly be nice to have a new sister to talk and gossip to, while our men are trapping and hunting."

"I am looking forward to it," responded Chokecherry Woman in sign.

There were cheers and whoops to go around, but it was not over yet, for Azariah and Howling Wolf knew that they had a story to tell around the campfires about their adventure. What was important, though, is that they were finally home with the people they loved and cared about.

24

As Rendezvous continued, everyone from both the Arapaho village of White Antelope and the Cheyenne village of Black Cloud were preparing for the impending wedding of Liam O'Reilly, also known as Raging Bull, and Chokecherry Woman, daughter of Yellow Hawk. Liam had asked Azariah to be his best man. While the wedding was being conducted in Cheyenne fashion, the Irishman wanted a tad bit of his own culture added to it, and he thought having a best man would do. Chokecherry Woman did not object, especially after how Liam explained to her how white men get married. Even though it was a little strange to her and her family, she liked the idea of the groom having a best man, while the bride had a bridesmaid. She believed that Liam couldn't have picked a better choice than Azariah to be his best man. Liam thought she should have a bridesmaid and asked her who she wanted. Chokecherry Woman chose Sweet Grass, who felt honored by her new sister to be chosen.

Crowfoot, the Cheyenne medicine man, presided over the service joining Liam and Chokecherry Woman's hands together. Bluebird and Little Fawn were standing not far behind their mother with their grandfather and uncle. Both girls were giddy and smiling from ear to ear as they watched their mother and new father go through the motions.

"Will you, Raging Bull," said Crowfoot in Cheyenne, "take Chokecherry Woman as your woman?"

"I will," answered Liam in Cheyenne.

The medicine man then turned to Chokecherry Woman and repeated the same question.

"I will," she answered.

With that, Crowfoot raised his hand in the air and looked up into the clouds. He asked for Maheo's blessing upon Raging Bull and Chokecherry Woman. When he was done, he said, "You are now joined together as one."

Everyone, Cheyenne, Arapaho, and a few trappers who were invited, whooped and hollered in unison for the happy newlyweds. Azariah shook Liam's hand, then gave him a bear hug, while Sweet Grass embraced Chokecherry Woman. Adam and Sara, who were both younger than Bluebird and Little Fawn, greeted them with hugs as if they were family.

As Liam embraced and kissed his bride, he noticed that He Dog and Black Cloud were chatting with one of the trappers who had been invited to the wedding. He appeared to be very young and not very tall, even by average white man standards. He didn't look to be more than five feet, six inches tall. He looked wiry and didn't seem to have a lot of meat on him, but there was something about the young man that, at least to Liam, showed grit.

He Dog and Black Cloud brought him over to meet the newlyweds. "Raging Bull," said He Dog in English. "This is Bent."

"Bent," said Liam with a questionable look as he offered his hand to the newcomer.

"William Bent," said the newcomer as he shook the Irishman's hand.

Liam was almost surprised at the small man's firm grip. It impressed him immediately.

"I have heard a lot about you, Mr. O'Reilly," said William Bent. "All of it good."

"I'm flattered," said Liam.

"Oh, and allow me to say congratulations to both you and your new bride," added William Bent, who doffed his beaverskin cap and bowed before Chokecherry Woman. Liam and Chokecherry Woman nodded their thanks. "I am told that you travel with a giant who rips out men's tongues with his bare hands."

Liam laughed before turning around and pointing to Azariah. "You mean this gentleman here?"

William Bent gasped and nearly fell backwards as Azariah approached him and offered a handshake.

"Goodness gracious!" shouted William. "Remind me not to get on your bad side."

Azariah laughed as he shook William's hand. "The name is Azariah Hancock," he said. "Treat me and my family the way you want to be treated and you won't be on my bad side."

"Fair enough," said William.

"In speaking of my family," said Azariah, "allow me to introduce my wife, Sweet Grass, and our children, Adam Bear Claw and Sara Sunshine."

As he did with Chokecherry Woman, William doffed his beaver-skin cap and bowed to Sweet Grass.

"It is a pleasure to meet you, William," said Sweet Grass.

"The pleasure is all mine, madam," responded William. "If you don't mind me saying, your English is better than mine."

Sweet Grass smiled at the compliment. "I have had a great teacher."

William Bent smiled at both Azariah and Sweet Grass before turning his attention to the children. "Tell me how old are these beautiful little angels from Heaven?" Adam walked up to William and offered to shake his hand, which was accepted.

"I am six years old," he said. "And my little sister is two."

William Bent was impressed with the young boy's handshake. "I have little brothers and sisters myself back in St. Louis who are around your age," he said.

"So what brings you to Rendezvous, William?" asked

Liam.

"For right now, selling my plews," answered William. "After that I hope to find a suitable spot to build a fort."

"A fort, you say?" said Liam with a raised eyebrow. The revelation also caught Azariah's attention.

"Yes, sir," said William enthusiastically. "I plan to make my fortune in the fur trade, but as a trader, not a trapper."

"You're thinking pretty big, ain't ya?" asked Azariah. "You don't look that much younger than me."

"True, Mr. Hancock, I am only nineteen years old," said William. "But you're never too young to think big, especially about the future."

"And that is why you're here," asked Liam.

"Me and my older brother, Charles," said William. "Speaking of which, I better go find him, knowing him he is probably getting too friendly with some poor chief's daughter."

Everyone laughed as William Bent once again congratulated Liam and Chokecherry Woman, before he went off to search for his brother.

"He can't really be serious," said Azariah.

"About what?" asked Liam

"Becoming a trader and building a fort," answered Azariah.

Liam just shrugged. "Like he said, it is never too early to think about the future."

With that, Liam put his arm around Chokecherry

Woman and they walked off together into the night as he held Little Fawn's hand and Chokecherry Woman held Bluebird's.

Azariah stood there for a moment, beaming with pride as he watched his best friend disappear into the night with his new family. At that moment a memory from his past appeared as thoughts of his own family entered his mind.

"Are you all right, my husband?" asked Sweet Grass.

Azariah smiled down at her. "I am. Just thinking, that's all."

"You still miss your family," she said.

Azariah was still amazed at how his wife could read his thoughts even after all these years. "You are my family," he said. "But I do miss my parents and my sister."

"It would be nice to meet them someday," said Sweet Grass.

"Yes, it would," responded Azariah. "If it is God's will."

Suddenly Azariah felt a tug at his pants leg, and he looked down to see his baby girl holding her arms out to be picked up. Azariah, with his big sledgehammer-sized hands scooped her up and gave her a peck on the cheek. She responded by grabbing her father's red hair and gently pulling it. Adam was standing next to his mother with Gideon, smiling at both his father and sister. With little Sara in one arm and his other arm around his wife, no words needed to be said as the young family and their dog walked back to their lodge to enjoy the rest of the night as well as the rest of their lives.

ABOUT THE AUTHOR

LeRoy A. Peters is a native of Clarksville, Maryland. After serving seven and half years in the U.S. Air Force, he attended Montana State University in Bozeman, Montana for three and half years before graduating with a Bachelor's Degree in History and a minor in Native American Studies. He first became interested in the fur trade after watching TNT's *Into The West* in 2005 and has read many biographies of famous mountain men such as John Colter, Jedediah Smith, Edward Rose, Jim Bridger, Joe Meek, Kit Carson, Thomas Fitzpatrick, Joseph Walker, John Simpson Smith, Lancaster Lupton and William Bent. He has also read biographies of many famous American Indian leaders such as Quanah Parker, Geronimo, Gall, Crazy Horse, Pretty Shield, Black Kettle and Dennis Banks. His is a fan of western authors such as Win Blevins, David Robbins, Richard S. Wheeler, Jory Sherman, Lane R. Warenski, D.L. Bittick, John Legg, B.N. Rundell and the late Terry C. Johnston. This is the second book in his trilogy series, *Edge Of The World*. He currently resides in Newark, Delaware.

Made in the USA
Coppell, TX
10 September 2023